Wagons to California

Wagons to California

Tom Curry

THORNDIKE
CHIVERS

This Large Print edition is published by Thorndike Press®, Waterville, Maine USA and by BBC Audiobooks Ltd, Bath, England.

Published in 2005 in the U.S. by arrangement with Golden West Literary Agency.

Published in 2006 in the U.K. by arrangement with Golden West Literary Agency.

U.S. Hardcover 0-7862-7749-1 (Western)
U.K. Hardcover 1-4056-3653-X (Chivers Large Print)
U.K. Softcover 1-4056-3654-8 (Camden Large Print)

The text of this Large Print edition is unabridged.
Other aspects of the book may vary from the original edition.

Set in 16 pt. Plantin by Liana M. Walker.

Printed in the United States on permanent paper.

British Library Cataloguing-in-Publication Data available

Library of Congress Cataloging-in-Publication Data

Curry, Tom, 1900–
    Wagons to California / by Tom Curry.
        p. cm. — (Thorndike Press large print Westerns)
    ISBN 0-7862-7749-1 (lg. print : hc : alk. paper)
    1. Wagon trains — Fiction. 2. California — Fiction.
3. Large type books. I. Title. II. Thorndike Press large
print Western series.
PS3505.U9725W34 2005
813'.52—dc22   2005008695

Wagons to California

CHAPTER I

River of Death

A merciless sun beat down on the wagon train. It was late summer and the breeze off the Nevada desert was stifling. The creak of ungreased axles in dry sockets grated on raw nerves. Now and then a man would grunt or groan, or a skeleton horse, unable to find subsistence, would stumble and fall.

They moved on, looking west, always hoping that the awful march would end. There were fourteen huge wagons in the train, and men and their wives and older children made up the party.

Bare, ugly hills, devoid of vegetation, hemmed them in. The Humboldt River ran east to west for three hundred miles and along it was the only central route for wagons going to California, land of promise. Greasewood and sage grew in the river valley, but it had been an exceptionally dry season and the scant grasses were burned crisp.

The Humboldt was a series of stagnant, scum-covered pools, so thick with bitter natural chemicals that not even animals dying of thirst could stomach it now. The earth had a whitish hue.

The emigrants tried to ignore the pitiful, rough crosses marking graves of men who had come before them along this deadly but vital route. Skeletons of oxen and horses and the remains of broken-down wagons showed that the 49-ers had come this way, and not so many years ago.

Now, though the Civil War was over and these Union veterans were making a new start in life. There was talk of a railroad that would stretch from ocean to ocean, but as yet it was only talk and did not help them. And even then hunger was nothing compared to the agonizing desire for water, water that would permeate every crying pore of dehydrated flesh.

A tall man with a powerful frame and a cropped black beard, his deep-set eyes gleaming, cursed and spurred his lame horse to the bank. It was steep, sliding white alkali. He dismounted and lay down to drink, but rose and spat out the stuff. His beaten horse would not even taste it.

Swearing, the man weakly mounted and dug in his spurs. At a walk, the half-dead creature moved through the dust cloud raised by the heavy wheels, bringing his rider to the leading vehicle of the slow-moving line of big prairie schooners that was strung out for half a mile.

"Colonel Gray!" cried the tall rider hoarsely, to the man who sat rigidly on the wide seat.

Dust coated Colonel Jason Gray's florid skin but there was a determined set to his cracked lips, despite the droop of his corn-colored mustache. Some of his natural stoutness had disappeared during the trip, but he still was a big man. His blue eyes were level and steady and his nose broad and generous. He had fought through the War as leader of a Pennsylvania line regiment and while he was a greenhorn in the West, he had a soldier's fortitude and an officer's solicitude for those in his care.

"What is it, Horton?" he asked.

"I want water!"

"There's none to spare beyond the ration," replied Gray in a kindly voice. "We have women and sick folks to think about, Horton."

"Yuh got two barrels in yore wagon.

Yuh're gettin' all you want yoreself, I'll wager!"

Gray frowned. He had stopped the horses to let them rest as he spoke with Horton.

His daughter sat on the box beside the colonel. Her head and most of her face were covered by a light shawl, in an attempt to keep out the choking dust, but her large, long-lashed blue eyes watched above its shelter, eyes that were the same shape and hue as Colonel Gray's, and she had her father's fair hair.

"I haven't had any more water than you have," Gray said evenly.

"That's true, Mr. Horton," the girl broke in. "Not as much, if you want to know. He's given much of his share to sick Mrs. Thorpe." She dropped the shawl to speak. Her oval face was attractive even though it showed the effects of grueling hardships on the Overland Trail.

"Never mind, Sue," Gray said gently. "Horton's sufferin' like all of us or he wouldn't say such things."

Horton scowled, his bloodshot eyes challenging as he pushed his mount closer and dropped his hand to the Colt at his hip.

"Yuh're an old fool, Gray!" he blazed. "If yuh hadn't stopped to let that sick woman die, we'd have been through by now. Give me some water, pronto!" The Humboldt Trail brought out the weakness of men as well as their strength.

"Don't!" gasped Sue, as Horton threw up his gun.

A man suddenly ducked from under the wagon. He had crawled underneath to come up beside Horton. He seized the fellow's wrist and twisted the pistol from his fingers. Infuriated, Horton kicked at him, cutting his arm with a spur point. The stalwart youth recoiled but did not let go of Horton's wrist, and by main force Horton was dragged from his saddle. The big young man pulled him in and lifted him high. The powerful Horton fought, screaming his rage, but he was helpless.

"Don't hurt him, Al," called Colonel Gray.

Men and women watched breathlessly from the wagons. The young man called Al tossed Horton onto a soft mound of sand. Horton lay there, gasping, swearing. "You all right, Colonel?" Al asked, grinning and Gray nodded.

Al ducked back under the prairie schooner, bobbing up on Sue's side.

"Here, Sue, look at this purty pebble I picked up for you a ways back." He gave her a smooth stone banded with black and purple streaks.

Sue loved colors and had a small box under the seat in which was a collection of unusual pebbles. She tried to smile as she took the new stone from Al, but she was suffering. Al thrust a canteen into her hand.

"I saved this for you, Sue. Drink it! I don't want it."

"Al, you mustn't!" she said, distressed. "You need it more than I do. You're doing heavy work, and two men's at that."

"Oh, I'm fine," he declared, but his lips were dry, his tongue thick.

Big, good-natured and even-tempered — the people of the train had never seen him really mad — Al Drew, a farm lad from Pennsylvania, wonderfully strong in body and spirit had been a tower of strength on the trek.

He wore dusty overalls and an old felt hat with a wide brim to shade his brown eyes. His hair curled thickly at the base of his tall neck and about his large ears.

Leaving the canteen on the seat, he went around to help Horton up.

"Take it easy, Horton," he advised. "We're all in the same fix but we'll get through if we stick together. Here, let me give you a hand."

"Get away from me, you clodhopper!" Horton's face burned with humiliation.

Color came into Sue's cheeks, now.

"Mr. Horton," she said sharply, "no one asked you to join our train. You insisted on it yourself. You needed food and help and we gave it to you —"

She broke off, as her father gently nudged her. Horton rode away.

Men's tempers ran short in the desert. Yet this was the first time a member of the party had threatened another with a gun.

"Indians!"

Gray's sudden warning made them forget Horton. Men dropped reins to snatch up rifles and pistols, as a horseman splashed across the stagnant Humboldt toward them. As he pulled up his lean-muscled, desert-bred mustang, however, they relaxed. He was alone and a bizarre-looking figure. They might have laughed, at another time.

He was a chunky savage, his torso naked, but he wore wide copper bands about his upper arms. He had on old leather pants and moccasins. Crowning a misshapen black-haired head, a battered high-topped beaver hat was cocked at a jaunty angle.

13

Under its brim gleamed intent black eyes, queer eyes, one partially crossed.

The party had been warned in Salt Lake City about the Indians who harassed the trail. The Diggers, the lowly inhabitants of the region, were not as a rule dangerous, for they were too busy hunting subsistence to fight much. They existed on crickets, ants and anything that would offer the slightest nourishment. However, roving Snakes and Utes sometimes invaded the Humboldt after loot. They were killers.

"Howdy!" cried the Indian. He raised a hand high, and came close to Gray. "Me Bad-eyes, white man's frien'. Spik fine Eng-lesh. Got tabac?" He grinned, showing broken, brown-stained teeth.

Gray handed him a package of tobacco.

"Obliged," he said. "Want water?"

"Yes, yes. How far?"

"Oh, two, three seventeen day."

The savage had no canteen. But he could move swiftly on his desert-bred mustang, and was no doubt inured to thirst and heat. He stared at Sue, then he grunted, his glance taking in the valuable wagon train.

Bad-eyes placed his right hand, the palm out, against his dirty breast and, looking at Gray, slowly moved his hand horizontally

14

toward the colonel.

"What's that for, Bad-eyes?" asked Gray.

"Uh? Oh, she say, goo'by."

The strange visitor jerked his rope halter, whirled, and with dust spurting from his snorting mustang's hoofs, he cut back across the Humboldt.

The sun was reddening ahead. The towering Sierras were lost in the dust haze. It was time to make camp for the night. Gray picked out a draw on the left, where there were some patches of grass not altogether burnt up, and where the horses could graze. They ran the wagons across the gap, and placed the stock inside the pen.

When the sun set, the air grew cold. Sometimes they shivered all night after the awful heat of the day.

Al Drew kept an eye on Horton, who throughout the trip had shown himself to be a bitter and ingrained selfish character. But Horton, after swallowing the little ration of water Gray doled out, lay down in the shelter of a jutting rock and went to sleep.

Drew made a bed near the Gray wagon. Sue and her father slept on the prized furnishings they were packing to California to set up a new home. Worn out, Al quickly drifted off.

It seemed to him that he had been asleep only a short time when he started awake. Yet the light of the new dawn was graying the Humboldt's dreary wastes.

He sat up, wetting his dry lips. Then he jumped to his feet. In the faint dawn he saw horsemen streaking at them from the river, wild men armed with rifles and bows, more and more spewing up from the bank.

"Indians!" bellowed Drew. "Everybody up and at 'em!"

The intention of the savages was obvious. As they heard Al shout, they set up a violent shrieking to terrify their prey, and opened fire. Bullets and feathered arrows spattered the wagons, kicking up dust and rock. The emigrants had had two guards set, but the Indians had come up during the darkness and hidden in the brush lining the steep banks. Al's warning had come before the startled greenhorns realized what was happening.

Drew threw up his revolver and began to shoot. Colonel Jason Gray leaped from the back of his wagon, his rifle ready. Other men were seizing weapons to fight for their lives and possessions.

"Take cover, Colonel!" shouted Drew,

over the din.

More and more bronzed killers swarmed from the river ditch. The men of the train shot at the swift-moving enemy, under the leadership of Colonel Gray who was a tried soldier and a good captain.

"Why, there must be a hunderd of 'em!" gasped Al Drew, squatted behind a heavy wheel hub.

There was a horde of the attackers. And some were big fellows, stained black with dirt and berry juices.

One of Gray's bullets knocked a savage from his horse. The colonel whooped triumphantly. He was a brave man, always an example of courage and fortitude to his friends. Most of the men in the train were former Union soldiers, trained to shoot. While they were tyros in the desert, they were good fighters.

Suddenly Gray gave a sharp cry, and staggered back. Drew leaped up, running to him. Sue Gray jumped from the wagon and bent over her father, who had fallen in the sand.

"Dad — Dad!" she cried.

Blood flowed beside the Humboldt.

CHAPTER II

The Scouts

Bob Pryor, the Rio Kid, lifted his handsome head, and his devil-may-care blue eyes carefully scanned the party of men below him, a group upon whom he and his two trail partners had come unexpectedly. It was a bright day, and the trained scout took care that no metal caught the sun. He flattened out again, looked back, and signaled with his hand.

One of his companions, Jim Bridger, wriggled his spare, long figure to Pryor's side.

"Mormons!" he exclaimed, his bony hand tightening.

"One feller down there looks like Bill Hickman," said the Rio Kid.

"Huh!" Jim Bridger said contemptuously. He had no love for the Mormons. In 1859, in their fight against the United

States, they had seized his fort and home. "Wonder what devilment they're up to now?"

The Rio Kid, Bridger, and Pryor's constant saddlemate, Celestino Mireles, were a hundred miles west of Salt Lake City, far from Brigham Young's haunts. However, the Mormon arm was long — and Bill Hickman was its crushing hand. The three scouts who had suddenly spied the man with his Mormon band were curious.

"I'll go down and speak to Hickman — he savvies me," said the Rio Kid. "Cover me, Jim."

Jim Bridger nodded. That was something he could do to the queen's taste. Most men were old at his age, but not this great explorer and scout. The years sat on him lightly, he was still powerful and agile in spite of his long career of Western Empire building, his abundant hair was brown, and his gray eyes as bright and shrewd as in his youth, now long past.

In the few years Bob Pryor had known Bridger, he had found the man equal to anything. He could keep up on the trail day after day, and match much younger men in standing hardships.

The Rio Kid was an athlete, too, a man hardened by four years as a cavalryman in the Civil War, and afterward in following the dangerous Western trails. He could keep going for days — and fight — with hardly any rest. But so could Jim Bridger.

In the Army, Pryor had been Captain Robert Pryor, dashing and debonair, an intimate of Custer and Sheridan and other great military leaders. Now he was the Rio Kid, restlessly seeking adventure that his bold spirit craved. He clung to many things reminiscent of the Army — the blue Army shirt he wore, for instance, and the dark whipcord pants tucked into carefully polished high boots. A cavalryman's campaign felt hat, too, which was strapped to his well-shaped head with its close-cropped chestnut hair.

Crossed cartridge belts supported two Colts, and he carried another brace in holsters under his shirt. So equipped, he could deliver twenty-five shots without reloading his carbine and pistols. And he rarely missed with any one of them, for he was a wizard with guns of all types.

His smooth bronzed cheeks glowed with health, and his chest was powerful. Broad at the shoulders, tapering to the narrow waist of the fighting man always in trim, he was the ideal height and weight for a cavalryman. And he was a fighter, for the Rio

Kid was known on the Frontier as icy cool in a scrap, a premier scout, and a man to have on your side. The commander's air about him impressed others at first contact, made them trust him.

He had made a noteworthy name for himself during the War, and since had increased his reputation on the Western trails. Though born on the Rio Grande, he had fought for the Union, and the terrible "Brothers' War" had uprooted him as it had so many other young fellows. He could not return to the tameness of ordinary existence, but must seek the peril that was tonic to him. All the more so, since on his return to his Texas home it was only to find the home gone and his father and mother — dead.

Young as Bob Pryor was, both he and Jim Bridger had discovered, soon after they had been thrown together, that they were ideal comrades in spite of the discrepancy in their ages, for they had much in common — especially their mutual love for an adventurous life. Most men who met Jim Bridger loved the man, and the Rio Kid was no exception.

He was a living tradition, Bridger. Since his early youth he had roamed the West. The Rio Kid was proud of the fact that this

21

friend of his had been the first white man to have looked on Great Salt Lake, two decades before Brigham Young thought of leading his Mormons there.

Bridger had discovered South Pass. In 1830, before Bob Pryor was born, Bridger had visited the Yellowstone, and the story he had spread of its natural wonders had been a national jest, and Bridger accredited with being the greatest liar since Munchausen — until his description proved to be fact. He had built Fort Bridger, the wilderness breathing spot for weary 49-ers, but the Mormons had driven him out, and now the Army held it.

In fact, no man could be said to have done more than Jim Bridger in opening up the western part of the young giant nation, the United States.

The other of the trio of scouts who were now observing the Mormons below them, Celestino Mireles, was a slim young Mexican whom Pryor had rescued from death on the Border. Right now Celestino was holding their horses behind a ridge, out of sight of the men they had seen, but at the Rio Kid's signal the young Mexican came forward, leading Pryor's dun gelding, Saber.

Mireles wore a high-peaked sombrero,

tight-fitting trousers and a short jacket, the garb of his countrymen. His thin, proud young face showed his patrician blood, and he was loyal to its last drop. He would follow his "General" as he insisted on calling the Rio Kid to perdition and back.

Mounting the dun, preparatory to accosting Bill Hickman and his Mormons, the Rio Kid skirted down the steep bank, and came out into the open. He was instantly sighted, and the men turned, watching him, gun ready, alert. The Rio Kid raised his hand in peaceful greeting, riding his horse back and forth a few times to set their minds at rest. Then he galloped toward them.

The horse under him was not prepossessing in appearance, but Saber, the mouse-colored dun, was a trained warhorse, a fighter in his own right. He was bad-tempered and intractable except with his rider. He had a mirled eye which rolled when he was angry, but he was the fastest thing on legs that Pryor had ever come across. The Rio Kid loved him like a brother, pampered him, and in return the dun gave him almost human understanding.

A heavy-bodied man pushed his dusty horse out from the group and sat watching

Pryor approach. The Rio Kid's eyes had not deceived him. He knew this man.

"Howdy, Hickman," he called, bringing the dun to a halt a few yards away. "I'm the Rio Kid. Savvy me?"

"Huh! I savvy. I don't forget easy." Hickman was coldly noncommittal.

His icy gray eyes pinned the scout. The wide, straight mouth, circled by a bristling beard and mustache, was grim in set. Curly, soft brown hair grew thickly about his big ears and fell over the expanse of his full, broad forehead beneath his straight-set flat-brimmed hat. The general expression of his face was cynical, pitiless.

He shifted his broad, buckskin-cased shoulders quickly, impatiently. His muscles were as supple as a cougar's. Physical strength and mental determination were here, in this executor of the Mormon law. He was legendary, dreaded by wrong-doers among the Saints and by outsiders alike.

The Rio Kid feared neither man nor devil but he had a healthy respect for Bill Hickman, chief of the "Avenging Angels," as they were sometimes called. Hickman obeyed orders strictly, just as a soldier would. He carried out sentences imposed by his superiors in Salt Lake City.

Behind him a score of men, most of

them mounted but several standing about something that lay in the salty sand of the desert, waited, silent. Bearded, unsmiling men whose eyes burned with a fanatical light. Their clothing was rough and plain, but all were heavily armed. They were Hickman's Mormon fighters.

"Yuh're a long ways from home, Hickman," Pryor said smiling.

"Who's that up there with yuh?" demanded Hickman.

"Oh, Jim Bridger — and some others." Pryor didn't expose his strength.

"So it's old Jim. Thought he was workin' for Dodge?" Hickman's voice was cool, and his gray eyes didn't waver.

"He is. I am, too. We just come up from the salt desert."

"Railroad routes, huh?"

Hickman looked sour for a moment. The Mormons feared the opening up of the far West. Suddenly he pointed a blunt stained hand back toward what lay on the sand.

"Yuh savvy anything about this, Rio Kid?" He kept his eyes riveted to Pryor's face, to see if he could detect any suspicious flicker.

The Rio Kid shoved the dun into the group, staring at the thing on the ground. It had been a man but the buzzards and

25

ants and wolves had been at work. Shreds of clothing, a gnawed old boot, and bones lay all about.

"No, Hickman," growled Pryor. "Who was it?"

Hickman spat a brown stream of tobacco juice.

"A Mormon and a good one," he said then. "Bishop Orson Watts. He was called by Brigham Young and started to Salt Lake City couple of weeks ago — he was missionaryin' in outlyin' parts. Carried tithe money with him, too. But his hoss never showed up."

"Been dead about two weeks, ain't he?" observed the Rio Kid. "It don't look like Indians to me, either."

"Not red ones, anyways." A dull-red flush crept up to the roots of Hickman's thick brown hair. "There's human coyotes attackin' the Saints on the Humboldt Trail for a time, too long a time, Rio Kid. I'm out of supplies now and my hosses are done in — didn't expect to be gone so long. But by all the livin' polecats in this cussed world I'll catch the men who're doin' it!"

He swung, and snapped an order.

"Put the bishop in that sack, boys, and we'll take him back and give him a decent burial."

Without speaking further to the Rio Kid, and with only a short nod, Hickman jerked his reins and started off. There was nothing more to be discovered here. Wind and weather had drifted the white salt sand into any tracks left by the Mormon bishop's killer.

The Rio Kid waved good-by and galloped back to Bridger and Mireles. Even as he told them what it was all about, Hickman and his men were moving slowly eastward for Salt Lake and home.

The scouts mounted and started for the Humboldt. They rode with light packs and traveled swiftly on their fine horses. They knew the secret waterholes and how to exist in the desert. All this barren, sinister land was familiar to Bridger, in particular, his old stamping-grounds. Hickman and his men were riding in the dust cloud they had raised, so the three scouts swung through the gap in the rocky ridges as they headed for the Humboldt.

By evening they were well along the trail.

"Looks as though that wagon train of greenhorns ahead had a slow trip and a tough one, Jim," the Rio Kid said, when they were following the tracks made by prairie schooners which had passed. "River ain't fit to drink."

"First I ever seen it," agreed Bridger. "The Overland Trail's a heart-breakin' trip to such folks, Rio Kid. I see the Forty-niners come through, in wagons, on hosses or pushin' wheelbarrows. Some just a-walkin', with packs on their backs all the way across! They'd have made the long march by the Platte, and they'd be nearly droppin' when they hit my fort, but they'd say, 'Well, it could be worse. Once we're over the Rockies, we'll be nigh there!' "

"They'd drag their wagons and gear up to Salt Lake and start a-rarin'. Only the salt desert busted their spirits mighty pronto. And the worst part of the run was still ahead — the three-hundred-mile Humboldt, and then the Sierras!"

"When General Dodge pushes the railroad all the way across to California, it'll be a heap easier for folks," said the Rio Kid. "What you think, Jim? This Humboldt Valley's the only route that looks good through here."

Bridger nodded. "The tracks'll run near it, for a good ways. I told Dodge that."

They camped for the night hidden in a draw. At dawn they were on their way, knowing they must get through quickly to save their horses and themselves. As they pushed on they could again read the progress of the slow wagon train which had passed days ago, for such vehicles made comparatively few miles in a march. A fresh grave told them that someone had died on the route. And the sign read to them that the wagon train had stopped for two or three nights, to bury the victim of the Humboldt trek.

The sun reddened the sky behind them, promising another day of dry, racking heat and flying dust.

They were about to pause for the noon rest, when the Rio Kid, riding in the van, cocked his ear alertly, stopped the dun, and signaled the others to be silent. Then he swung back to Bridger.

"Heavy firin', Jim!"

"Shore is! Injuns must have hit them folks, and they must be mighty weak by this time, too. Snake Injuns, I s'pose."

They hurried on, the Rio Kid in the van, with Saber running in the shifting white sand at a steady pace. The shooting grew louder after a couple of miles as the wind brought it to them. Shoulders of bare, ugly brownish-red rocks hid the trail ahead, but Pryor could place the fight.

He turned Saber up a narrow defile, Bridger and the Mexican following in his wake. Climbing a sliding rock pass, they reached a blunted ridge along which they could move, rather slowly, but on the height where they could observe the Humboldt.

"There they are!" cried the Rio Kid. "I can see some of the wagons, boys."

Bridger came up beside him and they surveyed the scene.

"Must have their stock in that draw," he said. "They're purty well protected for such folks, at that."

The big wagons were lined in an arc across the gap so that the horses were penned in, protected from frontal fire. Steep, jagged rocks prevented the Indians from getting around on the sides of the draw, except afoot, and exposing themselves when they tried to descend. The pilgrims were out of sight behind the wagons, while the attackers had taken up positions along the river bank.

From their vantage point, the Rio Kid and his companions could see the mustangs standing below, along and in the river, and the heads and lithe bodies of many savages lying up the steep bank, shooting at the whites.

"That's an awful bunch of redskins, Jim," observed the Rio Kid. "They must have had 'em pinned here a couple days, I reckon, from the looks of it."

Bridger agreed. "Looks like Snakes, what I can see of 'em. They're tryin' to draw fire and run them folks out of ammunition."

The Rio Kid dismounted, and took his carbine from the boot. Mireles and Bridger followed suit, and they moved up behind the crest, keeping out of sight of the Indians. They were finally blocked by deep splits in the rocks, and crept to the crest again.

The Rio Kid opened the ball.

CHAPTER III

The Humboldt's Toll

It was long range but the three scouts were expert marksmen. Pryor's carbine snapped viciously in the hot air and a savage flipped back in the stagnant Humboldt, quivering.

Bridger and Mireles let go an instant later, and two more Snakes showed they had felt lead.

"Let's stir up their mustangs, boys!" suggested the Rio Kid.

Slugs among the Indian horses started them rearing and fighting at the horse holders. The steep bank had shielded them from the wagon train's fire but from the ridge they were easy marks. Red-skinned fighters looked around anxiously, for loss of their mounts might mean death in the desert. Others sought to place the stinging new guns, that perhaps thinking some of the wagon train men might have worked up and around through the mazes of broken rocks.

Bridger and Mireles continued their steady, accurate shooting, but the Rio Kid paused when his carbine barrel became hot, and surveyed the general situation. He saw a tall, stalwart Indian, with his face and torso stained black and a bobbing feather head-dress, jump up and begin kicking at some of the prone fighters. He pointed at the ridge, and the Rio Kid could tell that the tall red chief was cursing his men and egging them on to attack.

Pryor took aim on him, and his rifle cracked.

"Nice shot!" complimented Bridger.

For the tall Indian had leaped into the air and come down on his back, groveling in the whitish sand. Another one in chief's head-dress ran to him, tossed him over a shoulder, and staggered across to the horses. He flung the chief across a mustang and leaped up behind him, spurring up the bank and dashing off along the screen of brush.

Slugs were too precious to waste on the chance of getting those two, so the Rio Kid turned his rifle again on the main gang.

The desertion of the two chiefs, the deadly fire from the ridge crest, settled the fight. Two Indians started the retreat when they turned and ran, jumped on their mustangs and galloped after the leaders. A whole section of the fighting line fell out then and panic seized the rest of the red killers. The rout became general. It was every man for himself and the devil take the hindmost, as they made their horses and rushed off.

"Fetch the animals around, Celestino," ordered Pryor.

"*Si,* General." The Mexican nodded.

Bridger and the Rio Kid found a way down the broken face of the cliff. The Rio Kid jumped the last few feet, landing in soft, hot sand. He came up and started to the people they had helped. He was smiling as he approached but as he saw the state they were in, the smile froze on his handsome face and pity struck his heart.

"Saved 'em from quick death, mebbe," he thought, "but I wonder if it was a favor!"

But he put this thought quickly away, his soul distressed at the condition of the pilgrims. There were women here, suffering with their men. Burning, red-rimmed eyes watched him. In the draw, their horses were complaining, crying out for water.

"Who's yore leader, gents?" the Rio Kid

asked, licking his lips.

He saw a dead man who lay near at hand. The body had been placed in a shallow grave but the men had been too weak, and too busy with the Indians, to complete the job. Others showed wounds, roughly bound. Lips were black, tongues swollen from thirst. A big young man — he was young, the Rio Kid knew, from his general make-up, though his face was white and drawn as though by age — pulled himself up and stood there, looking at the strangers.

"My name's Al Drew," he said hoarsely. "Our leader got wounded day before yestidday, when the fight started."

They had been here two nights and two days, then, thought the Rio Kid. He took in Drew's curly hair, the quiet brown eyes, the manly aspect of the youth, and liked what he saw.

Other men, still clinging to their hot guns, were red-eyed, suffering from thirst, too.

Hollow-eyed women and boys and girls in their early teens peered at Pryor from the wagons, and from the rocks behind which they had been sheltering. In their eyes he read the sudden, wild hope which sprang at sight of other white men, men who might have — water!

There were about forty of them, he figured at a quick glance. Bridger and Pryor carried canteens, and they had spare containers on their horses, which Mireles was bringing around the long way. But what they had wouldn't give more than a swallow or two to so many people. Bridger had already uncorked his canteen, and was beginning to dole out swallows of the warm but palatable water to eager throats.

A tall, powerfully built man with a black beard and deep-set wild eyes suddenly rushed from the rocks. He threw his arms around the Rio Kid's legs.

"Water — water!" he begged. "Please!"

"Women and wounded first," Pryor told him gently.

He was sorry for them all; all these thirst-crazed men here, and yet the big man was blubbering like a baby. It wasn't pleasant to see.

"Our water barrels got punctured by bullets," said Al Drew. "We ain't got but a few swallers left, mister. And we can't stomach the Humboldt."

"It's too low for drinkin', boy," said Bridger. "Makes yuh sick. I savvy."

Mireles was coming up with Saber and the other two horses. Knowing what lay ahead, Bridger, the Rio Kid and the Mexican shared the contents of their several canteens, reserving only one for future emergencies.

"Here's our leader, mister," said Drew. "He's Colonel Gray. He got hit mighty bad in the first rush."

The back of the prairie schooner he indicated was up. Some of the furnishings had been pushed out on the sand, and a bed made for the injured man. He lay on his back, staring up at the bowed ribs of the canvas top. Crouched by him was a hollow-eyed girl, with the same flaxen hair and blue eyes of the wounded man. Her lips quivered, showing the grief and suffering she was undergoing.

"Colonel Jason Gray!" exclaimed the Rio Kid, as he saw the wounded man's face more plainly.

The colonel's blue eyes rolled weakly. He was conscious and in obvious pain. His gaze fixed on the set, stern features of the Rio Kid. At last he whispered:

"Pryor! Captain Pryor!"

"You know my father?" whispered the young woman. "I'm Sue Gray."

"Yes, lady. He's a good soldier."

The Rio Kid's mind flashed back to the War, and once when he had been riding for

Custer. There had been a terrible battle in the woods of northern Virginia. The Union right flank had gone out, then the left. In the center had been a Pennsylvania regiment. The commander would not retreat. He had held the line, fighting the surging men in gray until the flanks rallied and counter-attacked.

The Rio Kid, then Captain Robert Pryor, had acted in the battle, getting the colonel's message back to field headquarters, to the stocky, silent general with the beard — Grant. After the battle, men had been decorated for their parts in it. The Rio Kid had been one of a group of officers receiving medals, and so had Colonel Jason Gray. Abraham Lincoln had come down from Washington to pin on the medals.

Then the War's duties had separated Pryor from Gray. He had however, heard of the colonel's splendid record.

From the look of them, many of the other sturdy Americans in this wagon train were ex-soldiers. They held themselves well, even in facing death.

Pryor climbed into the high wagon body and Sue made room for him beside her father. Jason Gray's face was drawn and drained of color, but they had been giving him swallows of water from time to time and he was fighting for his life with a soldier's will.

"It — it's in his right side, the wound," Sue said faintly.

The Rio Kid examined the injury, which had been roughly bandaged. It looked bad but he did not betray this in his manner. He called Jim Bridger to look at Gray. Bridger was expert at gunshot injuries.

When they had finished with Gray, the Rio Kid and Bridger stood in the center of the emigrants. Eager, pitifully hopeful eyes riveted to them, and they smiled and kept a cheerful front.

"Let's go see what the river water's like," said Pryor to Bridger.

"You can't even hold it down when you make tea with it," Al Drew told them.

"We'll have a look-see, anyway. Come on, Jim."

Bridger followed the Rio Kid to the Humboldt. The bank was several feet high, and there was scarcely a movement of the low water. Green scum had formed on the stagnant pools.

"The devil of a river!" growled Bridger. "In the spring, with the snow meltin' in the Rubies, it ain't so bad, Rio Kid. But this time of year it's so thick with alkali it's pizen."

"What yuh say about Gray?" the Rio Kid asked him.

"I'd say he has a fifty-fifty chance."

"Can he be moved? He's got to be, Jim! Them folks can't stay here. How much chance yuh give the train to get through?"

Bridger shrugged. "I'd say about the same as Gray's to stay alive and kickin'. I know of some wells fifty miles from here. I hope the water in 'em's drinkable."

The Rio Kid mentally agreed with Bridger. It was a toss-up whether they could bring the desperate greenhorns through. The horses were the main problem as far as transportation went. Pryor stood, staring across the Humboldt, the river everybody hated and yet must negotiate in order to reach the land of promise, California.

The signs of the Indians lay about, a few broken arrows, cartridge shells that had not been picked up in the retreat, gnawed bones of animals from which the meat had been chewed. Halfway down the bank, a small black object caught Pryor's trained eye. He slid down and picked it up, turning it over in his hand. Then he held it up so Bridge could see it.

"A white man's briar pipe, half buried in the sand, Jim."

Bridger shrugged. "Indian may have stolen it from a traveler."

"Yeah, of course. This is the spot where I winged that hombre though — the big leader. Then the other one run over to him. Did yuh notice how he moved?"

"Yeah, I did. Thought of it at the time, but seein' them folks sort of put it out of my mind. Acted like a white man, the hombre did."

A dark stain showed on the whitish bank, close to the spot where the Rio Kid had found the pipe. He cast back and forth, and then went down the bank. From the pool he pulled a hat, a battered old beaver hat. There was a bullet-hole through the crown, but high up. Whoever had worn it had evidently escaped but the slug had knocked the hat off.

"Might be a renegade white," he mused.

The Rio Kid stuck the pipe in his pocket and carried the beaver hat back with him. Al Drew was on his feet. The few ounces of water had revived him somewhat. He stared at the hat.

"Say, where'd that come from?" he demanded.

"Found it in the river," said the Rio Kid.

"Doggone, that looks like Bad-eyes' hat! I thought I seen his head a couple of times too, durin' the fightin'."

"Bad-eyes? Who's that?"

The Rio Kid listened carefully as Drew described the meeting with the Indian.

"I savvy," Pryor nodded. "This Bad-eyes was a spy for the gang. I reckon they make a habit of raidin' parties on this trail."

But the big thing was to pump new life into these people, and get them moving. He spoke to them, easily, so as not to alarm them any further.

"We must get started, boys," he told them. "Bridger says there are some good wells only fifty miles ahead. I'm goin' to send all the canteens that can be toted on a hoss up to the wells and bring back as much drinkin' water as possible. Celestino, that's yore job. Jim, will yuh lend yore cayuse? Yuh can drive a wagon, if yuh're willin'."

"Good idea, Rio Kid." Bridger nodded.

A lone man on the trail would be taking his life in his hands, with the Indians lurking near, but that did not deter these scouts. The Mexican was soon ready, and Pryor started him off. Mireles rode his own strong black and, leading Bridger's yellow cayuse, he galloped west along the river and soon was out of sight on his mission.

The Rio Kid doled out some dregs of warm water in the bottoms of the punctured barrels. He talked to the men, encouraging them, and they showed new hope.

"We're goin' to roll, boys," he finished. "We'll march this afternoon, and rest for the night. Tomorrer, Mireles'll be back with water. Look ahead to meetin' him and pick up yore feet. Get yore teams hitched up."

Except for Saber, the animals were all jaded, starved and suffering for water. But they must last till Bridger's wells were reached.

CHAPTER IV

The Mormons

The Rio Kid moved up and down the line, giving a hand here, a hand there. As he was helping one man get his teams hitched to the big schooner, he noticed Fred Horton, the black-bearded man, in the draw. Horton was savagely kicking and beating a dark-hided skeleton of a thing that had been a good horse at one time. Pryor couldn't bear to see an animal abused. He went quickly to Horton, and shoved the man away.

"That's no way to treat a hoss," he growled. "Here let me take a look at him."

"He's got to get up!" Horton insisted angrily. "I can't walk all the way!"

The Rio Kid knelt by the creature. Its brown eyes were dull, lifeless. He could see half-healed spur gouges in the flanks, the signs of abuse. The left hind leg was swollen to twice its normal size.

"Yuh ought to have yore head knocked off, Horton!" he snapped. "Mebbe yuh're a greenhorn and don't savvy hosses, but this one's completely done in."

He drew a Colt and quickly sent a bullet through the horse's brain. The creature lay flat on its side. He could see the neat brand on its flank, a star with a cross inside. He scowled at Horton.

"Start walkin'," he ordered. "There's plenty for yuh to do. Yore friends need all the help they can find. Buck up and act like a man."

Horton bit his cracked lip and his red-rimmed eyes blazed. "Yuh — yuh had no right to kill my hoss, yuh —"

The Rio Kid shoved him toward the wagons. Horton threw himself face down in the sand, shaking violently, sobbing. Disgusted, the Rio Kid seized him, dragged him to a nearby prairie schooner.

"Got room for this excess baggage?" he asked. He lifted Horton and pushed him in among the household goods.

He moved on up the line, busy with details. Al Drew straightened up from his work on a trace.

"I see yuh had a fuss with Horton, Rio Kid!"

"Yeah. What's wrong with him? He ain't

45

like you other folks."

"He's not one of our party, really. He caught up with us on the trail and we told him he could travel through with us. He seemed scared of the Indians by hisself, and he was out of food."

"I savvy."

Pryor had his mind filled with important problems. He forgot Horton, and soon started the train rolling, slowly, but rolling, west on the trail.

Jim Bridger drove Colonel Gray's wagon, while Sue stayed in the back with her father. Al Drew was driving the team belonging to the man who had died, and the Rio Kid, on Saber, assisted as he was required.

Choking dust rose under hoofs and heels. The heat was intense and thirst hung over them always. Thus had the 49-ers traveled the trail to California, fighting the desert, dying from Indian arrows and hardships, losing their wagons and goods en route.

Soon Bob Pryor came to know the individuals of the party. Most were Civil War veterans, men of Gray's regiment, and many answered to military titles. The second wagon belonged to Sergeant Tim and Becky Lang, with their two children.

Lang was a strong, naturally cheerful man of thirty-five, light of hair, with a broad, expressive face. He was able, efficient.

Sergeants, thought the Rio Kid, were usually good men. The noncoms were the backbone of an army.

Becky Lang was a courageous, dark-haired woman, and Tim Junior a tall lad of twelve. His sister Elizabeth was two years older.

Next in line came Corporal Zeke Burns, heavy-set, bearded. His wife, Edna, was pretty, slim, and with an uncrushable spirit.

Lieutenant John Fuller, small but wiry, followed. Then there were the Harrimans, the Bergers, and Sergeant Mike Reilly. Mike was the jester of the party, quick to laugh even in the face of death.

At the rear of the train came Major Rex Keith, who had been Gray's second-in-command, a sturdy, faithful man with a bald spot in his sparse, iron-gray hair. His three sons were young men, and his wife was silent, withdrawn, showing the strain of the trip. But all these women were grateful to be with their husbands after the separation of the War.

Somehow they made the afternoon march and camped for the night. The Rio

Kid brewed tea from the last dregs of stale, warm water left them in the barrels. When the sun fell they lay shivering in their blankets.

"Goin' to be an early winter, Rio Kid," grunted Jim Bridger. "Snow'll fall in the Sierras any time. These folks are mighty late comin' through."

"Huh! I'd hate to see this party caught in the mountains, Jim! Not many would live. We must get 'em to safety. I'm worried about Colonel Gray. That bullet's drainin' him."

"Yeah, but we can't take it out. He'd bleed to death from the joggin' of the wagon. Yet he'll die if he ain't fed and cared for right, and we ain't got the stuff to do it with here."

The Humboldt took its toll.

Mireles met them the next afternoon with filled canteens, and the welcome news that there was water in the wells ahead. The liquid revived the wagon train folks, and they pressed eagerly on.

When they reached the springs — dark, deep holes among brownish-gray rocks — buckets were brought up and the stock carefully watered. Men laughed, slapped each other on the back. Water made all the difference.

The Rio Kid sought Bridger. "Gray's slidin' fast, Jim," he said. "I'd hate to lose him, and it'd be a blow to his men. And his girl'll grieve her heart out."

Bridger glanced at him quickly. "She's a purty one, even on the trail. And that's sayin' a good deal for a woman."

"Yuh reckon we could get him to the Mormon's?"

"H'm. It'll take these slow wagons a couple weeks to make it."

"But our hosses could make it in days. S'pose we rig a rawhide and pole litter and make a stab at it? It's Gray's only chance to live."

"How about the rest of 'em?"

"We'll give 'em the route and they can follow. When Gray's taken care of, I'll start back and guide 'em to Stone's. He's got a big place."

"I'm with yuh. But our hosses are the only ones strong enough for such a job."

In the morning, the Rio Kid spoke to the assembled people.

"Bridger and I are goin' to take Colonel Gray to a ranch we know of in the Sierras. It belongs to a Mormon named Stone. It's a big place stocked with plenty food, and near the south trail. Foller in our tracks.

Major Keith, yuh'll have charge of the train in Gray's absence. Skirt the Sink, cut over to the mountains, and yuh can't miss the trail."

Rawhide, blankets, and tough wooden ribs cut from wagon-top bows were used by the Rio Kid and Bridger to fashion a litter for Gray. The horses, Saber and the yellow cayuse, shied violently from it at first, as the men carried it between them to accustom the animals to it. When they had trained their mounts to it, they were ready, and in the morning they tied the wounded man in the litter and started southwest for the trail to the Mormon's.

Gray's wound was tightly bandaged to prevent undue bleeding. Still the movement of the horses hurt him, and he gritted his teeth against the pain. They were taking a chance, but it was the only way they might save his life. Celestino Mireles came behind Bridger and the Rio Kid, carrying their equipment, and canteens of water. . . .

After three hundred miles from its source, the Humboldt turned south and petered out, ignominiously, in the desert. The Humboldt Sink was a ghastly, dreary waste. At times, in the spring freshets, a large lake would form, but now there were only dried reeds and a few scum-covered pools. On the east, the escarpment of the high Sierras rose sharply, so precipitously that only at a few points were there passes that men could scale on horseback or with teams. It was to the south pass that Bridger and the Rio Kid headed with their human burden.

Before them the mighty wall of the Sierras rose. The mountains were covered with evergreens and other growth, a tremendous and beautiful range separating the wonderland of California from the rest of the nation. The Sierras contained thousands of folds, wrinkles and side canyons not yet explored by white men. Sharp peaks reached to the low-hanging clouds as the Rio Kid and Bridger, walking now and leading their horses up the last miles of the steep trail, saw the Mormon's place before them.

The ranch was set in the beautiful vale of the Sierras. A clear, cold freshet rushed from the towering heights, offering more water than an army could use. Spaces had been cleared for crops, and the corn was ripe, the wheat fields acres of brown stubble. Big barns held fodder for cattle and horses through the winter months.

"Gray's still breathin'," growled the Rio

Kid triumphantly, as they wearily pulled up in the Mormon's yard.

The house, like all the buildings, was constructed of big logs cut from the slopes and chinked with natural mud plaster. It was large, running back to the north cliff against which it snuggled from the winter winds. Small windows, some with oiled paper in them, and shutters to close against the cold, broke the thick walls. Near at hand were storehouses with padlocks on the doors, woodpiles, corncribs, everything necessary to life.

Before they sang out, a large, stout man stepped from the open door of the house, and came toward them, beaming. He did not seem surprised to see them. He had a full brown beard, and a smudge of dirt on his nose, perhaps from handling a burnt log. The nose tip was as red as a cherry, and purple-veined cheeks showed above his whisker growth. Wrinkles were around his brown eyes, and he had thick wet lips. He was nearing fifty, and he had a hearty manner. He greeted the visitors in a bull voice.

"Well, well, it's Jim Bridger and the Rio Kid! How happy I am to see you again!"

They had come through the pass earlier, surveying for Dodge and the railroad.

"Howdy, Stone," said Bridger. "We got a wounded man here."

"Bring him right in, boys. My home is yores. We wondered what yuh was totin' — saw yuh comin'." Stone beamed.

Brown Indian faces peeked around the corners of the house as the men lifted the worn Gray and carried him into the big main room. Grizzly bearskins lay on the floor, and animal heads decorated the walls. There were hand-carved tables and chairs, big fireplaces. A strapping youth stood at one side, near him a big-game rifle leaning against the chinked log wall. He had a round head, uncombed thick brown hair, and his big red hands hung limp at his hips.

"Help the gentlemen, Vance," ordered Stone. "This is my son, boys," he said to Bridger and the Rio Kid. "He was out huntin' when yuh stopped last spring."

The scouts nodded, holding the heavy litter.

"Where'll we put him, Stone?" the Rio Kid asked.

"Over this way."

They refused Vance's proffered hand, and carried Gray through a dark inner hall to a side room, where they laid him gently in the bunk.

Stone drew a flask of whiskey from his back pocket and they gave Gray a drink. Vance Stone stood in the door, silently watching, and a door in the hall opened. Another young man, one who resembled Vance and Stone, came to stand behind Vance, staring at the new arrivals with open mouth.

"My boy, Hi," explained Stone, as they went back through the hall.

An open door drew Pryor's eye. He glanced through and saw a man lying on a bunk against the wall.

"That's Sam." Peter Stone, the Mormon, smiled. "The young jackass managed to shoot himself with his own gun while he was climbin' some rocks in the hills, huntin'."

Back in the living room, they consulted.

"We got to extract that slug from Gray, Jim," the Rio Kid said positively.

"Let him rest till morning," advised the old scout.

Mireles came into the house. He had rubbed down the horses, watered them and turned them into a corral. He bowed to Peter Stone, whom he also had met when the trio had paused for a few hours at the Mormon's some months before.

Stone sank heavily into his chair and

clapped his hands. Instantly an Indian squaw appeared, her moccasins soundless. For a moment the smile left the Mormon's face.

"Chow, pronto!" he snapped, and the squaw jumped back to the kitchen. Her beady black eyes had flicked to the heavy blacksnake whip hanging close to Stone.

"The man we fetched in," explained the Rio Kid, as he rolled a cigarette and relaxed, "is Colonel Jason Gray, an old soldier pard of mine, Stone. He was head of a wagon train and they were attacked on the Humboldt by a bunch of Snakes. Bridger, Mireles and I come along in time to help drive the Indians off. Gray's got a slug inside him and we brought him here to save him. He'll need to lie up for some time, and we'll guarantee yuh'll be paid for yore trouble."

Stone's thick wet lips clucked in pity.

"Pore chap! And where's the wagon train now, Rio Kid?"

"On the way here. When we get the bullet out of Gray, my hoss will be rested up and I'll start back to meet 'em and guide 'em in."

CHAPTER V

The Hunt

Next morning Bridger and the Rio Kid probed for the lead slug in Colonel Jason Gray. They found it quickly, extracting it with a minimum of pain. Gray fainted during the operation but his heart was strong enough when they bandaged him and covered him in his bunk.

By noon, Bob Pryor was ready to ride. Celestino Mireles and Jim Bridger helped him as he made ready.

"General — I weesh I could go weeth you," begged Mireles.

"Jim needs yuh here, Celestino, like I told yuh," the Rio Kid said. "I hate to leave yuh but I'll be back in a week or so with the folks."

"*Si, si!*" Mireles made no further objections. He had learned military discipline and was a good soldier.

Pryor mounted the dun. Bridger stared up into his bronzed, handsome face.

"Don't waste no time, Rio Kid. It's goin' to snow."

"Snow! It's mighty early, Jim!" But Pryor knew Bridger too well to doubt the old scout. "When?"

Bridger shrugged. "Within the week."

The Rio Kid nodded. He controlled the curveting, spirited Saber with one hand, and turned to wave to his trail mates, standing in the yard to watch him go.

The sun was warm, but a cool wind blew off the Sierras as he hit the downtrail, and moved around a pine-shielded turn which blocked the Mormon's place from his sight. Loose shale covered the trail, where it was not too steep for the shale to slide on down. Steep cuts at times fenced in the horseman, and the dun often had to be held back to keep him from overrunning himself.

The Rio Kid began, softly, to whistle an Army tune he and his mount enjoyed:

> Said the big black charger
> to the little white mare,
> The sergeant says yore feed bill
> really ain't fair —

He had made about a mile when his

alert eyes, scanning the way ahead, sighted several black shapes in the blue sky. They were not far away, those wheeling vultures. Something had died there, and the Rio Kid wondered what it was the scavengers were dropping to.

He quit his whistling. Saber sniffed, pricked up his ears. And the old wound in the Rio Kid's side began itching violently. The flesh had healed unevenly over his ribs, and some difference between the normal tissues and the cicatrized skin made it react that way — a warning to danger.

The Rio Kid jerked on his reins, and Saber slewed around as a bullet cut a chunk of felt from Pryor's Stetson brim, missing his skull only by inches.

He was moving back, close in to jutting rocks in the narrows, even as his Colt flashed to his hand, blaring a reply at the looming bluff which overhung the trail. Sharp-tipped rocks fringed with scrub brush made a perfect spot in which a drygulcher could lie, to ambush the trail. Pryor saw his bullets ripping the bushes, and smacking into the rocks, then Saber had whirled, back around the bend.

The Rio Kid could no longer see the bluff top, but neither could the hidden marksman see him. Leaping from saddle, Colt in hand, he hunted a way up and around, angry, but cool and collected in action.

The slope behind the steep bluff rose toward near-by heavy pine woods, so dense they roofed the brown-needled expanses below. The west side of the bluff was marked by huge chunks of reddish rock which had broken off through erosion. Crouched low, the Rio Kid began to climb, his body screened by the boulders. It was slow work but a deadly rifle was waiting, waiting just for a glimpse of him.

He paused at the crest. The bluff from which the killer had fired was about twenty-five yards to his right. He listened, but chattering birds in the pine forest and the distant roar of Stone's mountain rill interfered with his hearing anything else.

He tried an old trick, pushing his hat up for a moment into the sight of his hidden opponent. It drew no fire, but that didn't prove anything. Perhaps the drygulcher had recognized it as a trick.

The Rio Kid waited, seeking to strain out any sound of his enemy from the noises made by the woods creatures. The rocky slope between the pines and the bluff was not more than a hundred yards away, but in the minutes it had taken him to reach his position, the drygulcher could have retreated.

At any instant, then, he might expect a bullet. If the man had reached those woods he could work through them, come up on either side and have a clear shot at the man he wanted to kill.

The Rio Kid also was impelled by haste. Patient as he was by training, able to stalk animals and men to the death, in his mind was dread, dread for the fate of Gray's wagon train. If by chance it should snow before he reached them, the greenhorns might perish. He felt his responsibility keenly. He had undertaken to bring those people through safely, and he would die, if need be, to accomplish this.

He glanced at the woods. A thick pine at the edge vibrated violently, and he swung his Colt quickly. A large bluejay flew from the tree, screeching raucously.

"Here goes!" the Rio Kid thought, and bobbed up so that he was visible for a flash from the bluff.

Nothing. He gripped his gun and licked his lips. It was exciting, the expectation of death at any instant, of lead tearing through his flesh. He had been wounded plenty of times and knew the sudden, shocking power of a heavy bullet. The shrieking complaints of shattered nerves. Power left the limbs and instinct took charge, the instinct of self-preservation.

He glanced at the woods once more. In the dark evergreens there were tantalizing movements, tantalizing because they could not be diagnosed unless a bird or squirrel showed for a brief flash. Any one of them might mark his enemy's position, as the drygulcher crept in to try again.

Between the broken rocks and the bluff was a little dip. The Rio Kid leaped to his feet, watching ahead, then threw himself into the depression. No shot yet. Nothing to tell him whether his foe still held his position or had moved.

"I might have hit him," he thought, pressed flat behind the low crest.

He was now somewhat protected from the pine woods. He picked up a stone and tossed it into the brush-screened nest only a few yards before him. It rolled, stopped, then there was nothing more to disturb the natural peace of the scene.

The Rio Kid inched to the crest and sprang to his feet. Colt up and ready, the hammer spur back under his thumb, he rushed the rock nest.

It was empty. There were a few broken

twigs, and flattened moss where the drygulcher had recently been lying, and an empty carbine shell caught the light a few feet away. Squatted in the nest, he could look down on the trail to where he had been when fired upon. Turning, he saw the hole through which the gunman must have crawled, evidently leaving after he had missed his shot and his would-be victim had been creeping up through the rocks.

The Rio Kid heaved a deep sigh. He gazed toward the pine woods. No doubt that his unidentified assailant had retreated into them.

The area between the bluff and the woods was open and offered little cover. Gun ready, he jumped to his feet and, bent low, ran full-tilt for the woods.

When he reached the trees he threw himself down, his breath coming fast. His quick eyes searched the shadows of dense thickets. Inside the screen of the first trees — where they had the full benefit of the sunlight they could develop to their bases — the rough slope was carpeted by the dropped needles of a century. Dry brown trunks and dead branches interlocked.

The place was alive with birds and squirrels. They scolded him, and their shrill voices rang through the woods.

The Rio Kid was convinced now that the drygulcher had not stopped to fight it out, once he had missed his kill. He had run away and somewhere in the great forest he was lurking, creeping on now and then, looking around fearfully to see if he was being trailed.

The Rio Kid shook his head. "Take me all day to hunt him out," he muttered. "I got to get back to the folks."

He hurried to the trail and, picking up Saber, rode on.

The Sierra country was startlingly beautiful, and stirred the heart. But man had brought death into these lovely mountains. Savages, early trappers, and Spaniards, had fought in them. Now a different breed of killer was taking over.

A mile down the mountain, he sighted a dead horse lying across his path. So that was what the vultures were after. Several of the awkward things rose from the carcass, screaming at the rider, their huge wings beating the air as they flew to the nearby trees. The Rio Kid stared at the dead animal. It was a bay, with a large frame.

"Why, that looks like Colonel Gray's lead horse!" he exclaimed, and jumped down.

The bay had picked up a little flesh over his ribs from grazing and watering after the awful Humboldt had been passed. But he showed signs of horrible mistreatment. Open spur gouges now were covered with flies, and there were cruel whip marks on the horse's flanks. He had been driven to death by his rider, up the steep slopes of the mountain.

"Whoever it was deserted the train," the Rio Kid growled, and it did not take him long to reach a conclusion as to who that was. "Only one hombre in that bunch who'd treat a hoss like this, then try to get another by drygulchin' me!"

Then he thought, "S'pose an Indian stole the hoss, though. That's possible. I've got to make shore. And I'll have to warn Bridger and Stone."

Reluctantly, for he was eager to return to the wagons, he turned and rode back to the Mormon's. It was slow going as the dun strained forward, head down, sliding on the shale. Reaching the last crest, the Rio Kid started around the turn. Saber was sniffing, and the rider suddenly spied a man limping into the dip of the vale in which Peter Stone's ranch sheltered.

The Rio Kid pulled back, and dismounted. Getting up to the line of trees along the road, he hastily followed the tall man who had sighted Stone's and was eagerly pressing toward the place. Once he glanced around, and the Rio Kid recognized Fred Horton's bearded face.

"I knew it!" he thought. "He stole the best hoss in the train and deserted 'em. He gored the hoss to death, then tried to drygulch me and take Saber! Cuss him, he don't stop at anything!"

On the Humboldt, Horton had been sniveling, fearful. But water and food, after the desert, had brought back his strength.

The Rio Kid came in from the trees, while Horton was rounding the path to the Mormon's. Peter Stone and his two sons, Vance and Hi, were standing near the big barn, watching Horton approach. The Rio Kid moved around until he had the building between himself and Horton. He did not wish to give the desperate man a chance to pick him off with the carbine slung over his shoulder.

As he quietly tiptoed around the barn, he heard Horton's hoarse voice ask:

"Are you Peter Stone, the Mormon?"

"That's me. Who are you, stranger?"

"My handle's Fred Horton. Glad I got here. I didn't savvy I was so near yore ranch when my hoss collapsed. I know of yuh, Stone, and I got somethin' important to tell yuh."

"Have you?" replied the Mormon coolly.

The Rio Kid stepped around the corner of the barn and jammed his Colt into Horton's back ribs.

"Reach!" he commanded grimly.

Horton was violently startled. He threw up his hands, and the Rio Kid ripped the carbine from him and flung it aside. Fearfully Horton glanced at him and his face worked spasmodically as he recognized his captor.

"Rio Kid! What's the matter? Why —"

"Dry up, Horton." Pryor's deft hand lifted a gun and a knife from the man's belt, then he moved around in front of him. There was an icy glint in the Rio Kid's eyes.

"You polecat, Horton. Yuh tried to drygulch me on the trail. Yuh didn't savvy yuh was so close to the ranch and yuh wanted a new hoss — after yuh'd beat Gray's to death."

"No, Rio Kid! I thought yuh was a bandit! So help me, that's the truth."

"Yuh don't know what truth is, Horton! Yuh stole Gray's lead hoss and deserted the wagon train. I wouldn't put it past yuh to have killed one or two of them wagon train folks before yuh got away."

"I bought that hoss from Sue Gray!" Horton protested wildly. "I tell yuh I didn't savvy yuh! I was a fool with an itchy trigger finger. Then I run away when yuh fired. . . . Please don't shoot me." He appealed to the Mormon. "Don't let him kill me, Stone!"

As the Rio Kid continued his search of Horton he was remembering that Al Drew had told him, the black-bearded man had joined their party on the Humboldt.

There was a fat wallet in Horton's inside shirt, along with a small notebook, a black-leather diary. A large gold watch was hidden in Horton's side pocket, and when the Rio Kid extracted it, Horton shook as though with ague.

"Yuh thief!" he snarled. "Give me back my property!"

The Rio Kid slapped him, and Horton subsided.

Pryor stepped back a couple of paces so that Horton couldn't jump at him. He examined the watch. It was an expensive item, and he pushed a catch, so that the back clicked open. A name was engraved on the inner heavy gold cover. "Hey, Bridger!" sang out Pryor, "come here!"

"What is it?" demanded Peter Stone.

Jim Bridger and Celestino ran out at Pryor's call, to his side.

"Look, boys," he said. "Remember the dead Mormon bishop, the day we ran into Bill Hickman?"

He pointed to the name in the watch.

ORSON WATTS

CHAPTER VI

Storm

Pryor's heart was filled with cold fury. Now he could reconstruct the ugly career of Fred Horton, along the trail.

"Yuh killed Bishop Watts the way yuh tried for me, robbed him, and took his hoss!" he accused. "Then yuh lit out for the Humboldt. Yuh was short of food, and yuh beat that poor hoss to death gettin' there. The folks in the wagon train helped yuh, fed yuh, and protected yuh on the way, and I savvy how yuh repaid 'em."

He examined the black notebook. Orson Watts' name was inside it, and was filled with notes in a fine handwriting. The Rio Kid read:

Brother Orpheus Brown has a complaint against Timothy Fallow. It concerns three sisters,

69

all of whom Brother Brown desires to marry, while Brother Fallow says Brother Brown is a hog.

Tithe collections here not as much as should be. I gave the brethren a stern admonishment as to their duty.

Near the center of the book several pages had been roughly torn out.

The Rio Kid realized that he was reading a confidential report by Bishop Watts, no doubt for accounting to Brigham Young on his return to Salt Lake City. Then he saw the name:

PETER STONE

The notation below the name read:

Brother Stone lives a long way from Salt Lake City. Tithe matters do not seem so vital to Mormons who dwell so far from the center of the world. Now, I have made careful inquiry of several survivors, and —

That was where the pages had been torn

out and the remaining leaves in the book were empty.

Peter Stone was glancing over the Rio Kid's shoulder. Pryor passed the watch and book to the Mormon.

"Take charge of these, Stone. They belonged to Bishop Watts and I reckon the wallet did, too."

Stone scowled at Horton. The Rio Kid deliberately pouched his Colt.

"I can't kill a man in cold blood, Horton," he said. "Not even a snake like you. Pick up yore pistol and start shootin'. First try is yores."

But Horton refused. He knew the Rio Kid's speed. His tongue licked his bearded lips, his wide eyes searched Stone's face. Pryor stepped in and struck Horton in the mouth, smashing his lip against his teeth. He hit the man again before Horton crumpled, sobbing, at his feet.

"Get up and fight!" shouted Pryor.

He would not kill or beat a man who wouldn't fight back.

"Pull him off me, Stone!" begged Horton. "Brigham Young wants to know —"

Stone stepped closer. "Brigham? He is my friend and Leader, Horton!"

Horton grew silent as the stout Mormon

71

glared down at him.

"No doubt that this man is a killer and rascal, Rio Kid," Stone said then. "A fugitive who must answer to Mormon justice for his crimes. I'll take charge of him and see he gets what he deserves. I have a lockup where I keep thievin' Indians at times. I'll hold him in it."

"A good idea, Stone. I'm in a powerful rush now, to get back to the wagon train. If he killed anybody there I'll see he's hung myself."

"And I'll furnish the tree and rope," Stone said grimly. He kicked Horton. "Get up, you . . . Hi, Vance, throw this critter into the dungeon."

Stone's strapping sons seized Horton and lifted him as though he were a bag of feathers. They ran him across the yard to a windowless, thick-walled log shack, back to the cliff, threw Horton inside, and slammed the door, snapping on a big padlock.

Pryor, having dealt with Horton, took his leave again. Shrill whistles brought the trained dun running to him, and he mounted, swung east. He rode through the rest of the afternoon, making good time down the steep slopes. At dark he camped, hidden off the trail with the dun.

He woke to a gray dawn which did not lighten much. The Sierras were capped in clouds, and as he resumed his journey toward the wagon train, the overhanging sense of dread grew. He tried to whistle it off, but he could not shake that urgency to hurry, hurry.

He was well down the gap when night again overtook him. He rolled in his blankets but a dank chill pervaded the world and he was cold when he fell asleep. Starting awake, he found that his blanketed form was covered with wet, clinging snow, three inches of it, and the sky was black. The aspect of the world had changed. It was ghostly as the big flakes silently fell, the billions of tiny crystals forming into a tremendous mass.

"Bridger shore was right!" he muttered, sitting up.

It was 3 a.m. He found some pine twigs sheltered in a near-by grove and lit a fire, fixing breakfast. He smoked, hoping the snow might stop. It was early in the season, even in the Sierras, for big storms.

As soon as he could see his hand before his face, he saddled Saber and got back on the road. The snow was thick. He could not see far ahead, and soon man and horse were covered with the sticky white, and Saber's shod hoofs slipped and skidded. The earth was not frozen under the snow, and mud quickly formed.

"Wonder if they're in the mountains yet?" thought the Rio Kid. . . .

The wagon train people who occupied the thoughts of Bob Pryor, the Rio Kid, were in the mountains. They had reached the foothills the day before, and were planning to go on to the higher Sierras at daybreak.

It was about the time the Rio Kid awoke beneath his blanket of snow that Al Drew also awoke in the chilly night. It was, he thought sleepily, much colder in the mountains than along the Humboldt. The shapes of the big wagons, drawn into a ring for defense in case of Indian attacks, stood out vaguely against the faint glow from the campfire. A man coughed nearby — Mike Reilly, on night guard.

Drew suddenly realized that he was covered with snow. It worried him. It was still snowing, too, the flakes melting on the warmth of his cheeks. Most of the people slept in the wagons, atop their belongings, but Drew preferred the open air.

He got up, shook the snow from his blankets, and went over to Reilly, one of whose duties as sentry was to keep the fire alive.

"Hey, Mike! I don't like this!"

"Oh, 'tis nothin'," said Reilly cheerfully. "Jist a bit of dew from heaven, me boy. By noon you'll never know it snowed."

But the world was white with inches of snow when they had finished breakfast and hitched up for the day's march. They had made good time to this point, following the Rio Kid and Bridger, and their horses had quickly picked up with fodder, and plenty of water.

They were climbing the steep escarpment which would lead them to the higher Sierras. The day before, the great mountains had towered over them, clad in many colors — reds, grays and purples of rocks, various greens of trees, and other hues. Now they showed only a shimmering whiteness, save where some jagged sentinel rock had disdainfully cast off the snow. Even the trees were covered with a sticky blanket.

"Reckon yuh were right, Mike," Drew said in mid-morning. "Looks like it was stoppin'."

The snow had thinned so they could see farther ahead, but the sun failed to come out. As they drove up the slopes, the hard-working horses slipped and the big wagons skidded frighteningly. Under hoofs and wheels the wet earth quickly churned to mud.

Everybody was out, to lighten the loads as far as possible, and all who could, lent a hand pushing up steeper places. Sue Gray was driving her father's wagon, bravely doing her share, anxious as she was about her father, hoping against hope that the Rio Kid could save him.

Everybody was glad that Fred Horton, the ugly-tempered, black-bearded man they had helped on the Humboldt, had left the train. They had lost a horse, but they considered it worth it, since Horton was gone — good riddance.

Often they had to stop to let the steaming animals rest. Because of the snow they had to hook up ropes at times in order to negotiate the slides. After the noonday rest it snowed harder, and they could not see far ahead. The trail was completely hidden.

In the middle of the afternoon they came to a spot where Major Rex Keith could not decide on which branch of a fork to take. Drew, Keith, and several of the other men gathered in front of the stopped train, staring at the two paths offered. Both were choked with snow.

"Which way, boys?" asked Keith.

"I'd say the right-hand branch," said Reilly.

"It's bigger and it runs due west," agreed Zeke Burns.

Sergeant Lang spat a yellow stream onto the snow.

"I vote for the left, gents."

"But it swings off too much south," argued Keith. "However, we'll vote on it."

Drew was confused, uncertain which way was the right one. But the larger gap, running due west, seemed the more likely. The left branch was steep for wheels and halfway up made a sharp turn into which the snow had drifted deeper than a man's height.

The emigrants voted on the bigger opening and Sue Gray's team started into it, the horses straining mightily. In the vehicles were packed their precious belongings, all they had saved from their homes in Pennsylvania, the only ties left, and with which they hoped to make a start in California. None were rich. The soldier pay of the men had been invested in the equipment which was to take them through.

After they had pushed and worked the prairie schooners through the narrows, the country opened out. They were pleased, for the slope was not steep and they were able to make better time. Reaching the top of a long but gentle hill, with great mountains towering on both sides, they moved over the crest, and for two miles it was downhill. They crossed a swift-running, but shallow mountain torrent, its water cold as ice.

"Yuh feel better'n in the desert, boys!" exclaimed Al Drew. "Cold weather always bucks a man up!"

They were not yet frightened.

"The Rio Kid'll find us, soon," said Major Keith confidently, "and help us to the Mormons."

Over the next slope, they were presented with a towering white monster of a mountain, whose shoulders joined to other less imposing summits. They paused, staring at this massive wall, aware they could never surmount it without long hours, perhaps days, of pulling with ropes. Snow covered the mountains, and the evergreens tenting the ground. Big pinnacles of jagged, magnificent rocks stuck to the somber sky.

"There's the gap — right there!" cried Mike Reilly, whose eyesight was keen.

Almost hidden from them by a toelike

spur of the mountain was the gap through which the rivulet came. They passed it, sometimes with wheels in the water, sliding on the rocky bottom. The wildness of the scene staggered them. The country opened out into a vast park, broken by patches of woods and rocks. It was almost dark when they crossed it, and camped for the night by the stream.

It snowed more during the night, enough to cover their back tracks. The sun came out, and they were enheartened, believing the storm to be over.

They followed the brook for several miles after their quick breakfast, but it swung north and disappeared between two precipitous cliffs. Drew went ahead, wearing the rubber boots he had in his wagon pack. His feet were nearly frozen, when he returned to report the way was altogether impassable for teams.

They left the brook and pushed west, gaging it by the position of the yellow sun. Now the light blinded them, shining on the virgin snow. More mountains lay ahead, and they were growing weary of the trail-breaking for the wagons, of hauling and pushing. Even Reilly fell silent, his jokes bringing no laughter as the worried greenhorns struggled on.

"We took the wrong turn back there," Drew kept thinking but he couldn't admit it.

To back-track would be fatal. The strain of running the wagons through the snow was too great.

CHAPTER VII

Share and Share Alike

By nightfall the wagon train people were in a maze of canyons, thousands of folds and creases in the white hills. The noon sun had started the snow to sliding, and the biting wind of the late afternoon shook it off the trees and slopes.

They bore west as much as the land permitted them. And they progressed, worn with the fight against the country and the storm.

The third afternoon, they were moving up a narrow canyon. Reddish-brown cliffs hemmed them in, and brush and trees grew thick in spots.

Al Drew, breaking trail ahead of the horses, came to a little crystal-clear brook. It turned to the left and disappeared in a slit in the precipice. They kept along the stream, bound by the cliffs. And here they reached the end of the trail.

Drew stood, craning his neck up at the terrible height which shut off the blind canyon from the rest of the world. It was well over a thousand feet high. In places there were ledges, but not even a mountain goat could have scaled the sheer, often undercut walls. Nor was there any gap. The train was boxed, save for the brush-covered entrance through which they had come.

They took counsel.

"It's mighty late and we better camp till mornin'," advised Major Keith.

None of the weary men disagreed. They beat down the loose snow, unhitched the cold, dispirited horses, watered them and gave them a little grain, the last of their store.

There were evergreen branches and dead wood and they had a roaring fire. Drew, poking near the cliff, hunting good logs, saw a dark gap overhung by snow. He investigated, and then went down to his friends.

"There's a big cave up here," he reported. "It's dry inside. We could fix a mighty nice camp in it."

Keith, Reilly and others went up to look at the cavern. The mouth was drifted with snow but they brushed it aside, and the entrance was four or five feet high at the center. It opened out into a large, roomy chamber, carpeted with loose, sandy dirt. They could not see the back reaches. They were lower, and cut off by protruding arms and rock. There was plenty of room for all the men and women and children, and the fire built at the mouth warmed the air.

Drew and his companions carried in food, to cook for supper. They had only necessities and not many of these — flour, which could be made into bread in portable Dutch ovens, salt, a bag of sugar, a little tea, barrels of salt pork and dried beef.

During the long trip from Missouri they had consumed a large proportion of their stores, and in Salt Lake City prices had been so high that they had been unable to restock. They had counted on wild game but had seen scarcely anything save rabbits and tracks. The game stayed away from the trail and it took expert hunters to track it down.

They slept warm that night, in the cave, divided by canvas into sections for men and women. During the night it began snowing again, and their wagons were drifted high when they awoke. The second half of the storm had struck.

The people stared out. Their back-track was covered. The horses were shivering, standing huddled together, waiting for attention.

"I'm in favor of stickin' here, where we got some shelter," growled Rex Keith, his eyes grim as he looked at his friends. "Even if we manage to get back, boys, to where we made the wrong turn, we'll never make the summit in snow. If we stay where we are, mebbe the Rio Kid'll fetch us help."

"Yeah, that's it!" cried Drew heartily. "That's the smart thing, Major. The Rio Kid's shore to find us."

He spoke enthusiastically. The women and children were listening, watching, their eyes haunted with anxiety.

Later Drew went out with his rifle, to hunt. But he could not move far without snowshoes, and he saw no game. The world was again entirely white, save for the breaks afforded by the cliffs. That afternoon Drew went to the shallow stream, to fetch buckets of water. Ice crusted the edge and he broke it off with the long-handled shovel he had brought along.

It was difficult dipping the pails in the few inches of water. He couldn't get a pailful. He meant to dig out a pool to save time, in front of the cave, and scooped out some of the reddish sand, heaping it to one side. It muddied the water but the current quickly carried it away.

Drew stared at the sand he had brought up. He stooped, and curiously examined little yellow flakes which stood out against the reddish sand. Digging around in the small heap, he found two or three chunks of it.

"Hey, Major!" he called. "Look at this!"

Keith and Mike Reilly came over, to see what Drew had discovered.

"Gold!" gasped the Irishman.

They stared at one another. None had ever seen placer gold but they had heard the wild tales of 'Forty-nine. The discovery excited the emigrants who hurried out with shovels and began digging along the brook. The snow had stopped, and the sun was showing when afternoon came.

That evening they sat near the big fire the men kept going, from wood cut off the stream bank. Eyes shone in the red glow, and for a time they forgot their dangerous plight. Gold was the theme. All had picked out a little during the hours they had worked.

"This belongs to us all, share and share alike, boys," said Keith. "Jason Gray owns a hunk, fair and square."

They agreed, and they lay down to sleep, dreaming of riches, of gold.

Drew had rolled in his blankets well up in the cavern, near the wall. In the morning, when the faint light showed in the mouth of the cave, he awoke and his moving hand touched something which made him start.

He heard a weak, dry rattle, and was up and away in a sudden, convulsive leap. A six-foot rattlesnake had shared his bed with him. But it was torpid, from the cold, and only slowly opened its mouth, showing the deadly fangs. Drew despatched it with his shovel, and wiped the sweat from his brow.

"Dog it, the warmth of the fires must have stirred it up! Wonder how many more are winterin' back here?" He stared at the blackness to the rear of the cavern.

He lighted a pine torch, and with the shovel ready, started back to explore. The sandy floor slanted down, and after he had passed several jutting fingers of dark red rock, he found it widening, branching off in a half-circle before him.

It was warm in there, and the air stale. He discovered a nest of serpents, rattlers, young and old, and killed them as a precaution. His torch was burning low, and he turned back. The light caught on some colored pebbles near the clay walls and he picked up a few and put them in his pocket.

The torch burned out, but he could see the way ahead. As he neared the outside room, he heard the sound of low sobbing. Turning aside, he found Sue Gray huddled outside the canvas wall which had been hung on poles to separate the men's from the women's quarters.

Everybody else was out near the fire, eating breakfast.

"Sue!" he said, distressed. "What's wrong? Why yuh cryin'?"

He knelt at her side, smiling into her face. She meant the world to him but he had never dared to tell her so. He was humble before her, finding it impossible to voice his feelings.

She bit her lip, and tried to compose herself.

"I . . . we're lost, Al, lost! I hoped to be with Father by this time. I don't know whether he's alive or —"

"He's all right, Sue. I feel it in my bones! The Rio Kid got him through safe and sound." He went on earnestly, "Don't worry. We got shelter here. We could stay here all winter if need be."

"We have no food — only enough for a week or two. I don't care about myself, but Father needs me."

"We can hunt, find game," lied Al. "And when the spring comes and we get free, we'll be rich, with that gold. Don't worry." He put his hand into his jacket pocket, and drew out the pretty pebbles he had brought for her. "Look, I picked these up for yuh, Sue, back in the cave."

They interested her. The shaft of light from the cavern mouth caught their colors. Some were reds, others blues and greens.

"They are pretty, Al! You know why I'm saving them? When we get to California I'm going to make dresses for ladies. I can trim hats and make ornaments with these, can't I?"

"Shore yuh can. There's more back inside, and we'll collect 'em."

She stopped crying, wiped her eyes, looked up at Drew, and smiled. She had been brave throughout the journey, but was hardly more than a child, just in the flush of young womanhood.

"You're good, Al, so good. I couldn't have stood it all without you."

She put her hand in his, and his heart gave a mad leap, wild with joy and hope.

For a time they looked straight into one another's eyes, then slowly their lips met.

The grim Sierras hemmed them in, trapped them in untracked myriad creases and folds. But even facing death, love and life fought bravely on. . . .

In another part of those same mountains, at that moment the Rio Kid also was fighting on. Blindly he staggered up the steep trail. He was walking. The worn dun could not negotiate the snow and mud and sharp rises with a rider on his back, and Saber had fought gallantly against the storm with his rider, as they had sought the wagon train.

When the second half of the storm had come, the Rio Kid had been down out of the mountains, and as yet the wagon train had not shown. He had missed it by twelve hours. He had slid down the drifted turn at which they had taken the wrong track the morning after Keith and his friends made their fateful decision. Snow covered all sign.

He was out of provisions, and no horse could last forever without proper rest and attention. The Rio Kid was too shrewd to peter out in a useless hunt. He guessed that somehow, the train had taken the wrong turn.

"Mebbe there'll be a clear spell before the big snows come," he considered. "I'll go back, get Bridger and Stone to help, and we'll find 'em. The folks can last a long while at their wagons."

The trip back almost finished both horse and rider, and the Rio Kid, teeth gritted, his handsome face chapped dark by cold, dug ahead on the slippery way, pulling at the reins to help Saber keep footing.

A harsh voice came suddenly out of the snowy air.

"Halt, cuss yuh, or we'll blow yore consarned ears off!"

Pryor stopped, his eyes rising to the bluff. He was close to the Mormon's. Vance and Hi Stone gaped at him, rifles up.

"Don't shoot, boys!" he called. "It's the Rio Kid!"

"Dog me if it ain't," growled Vance. "Figgered yuh was coyote bait by this time. Go on, Bridger's cryin' for yuh."

Vance seemed to be laughing at the Rio Kid. But Pryor moved on, glad when he reached the stamped ground outside Stone's. Mireles dashed out to seize his hand, shouting in joy. The Mexican took care of Saber, while Pryor walked into the house.

Peter Stone glanced up at him dully, from his chair by a blazing log fire. A bottle lay empty by him, and his eyes were bloodshot as he blinked.

"Howdy, Stone," the Rio Kid greeted. "I didn't find the train. Storm covered their tracks. Where's Bridger?"

The fat Mormon's lips were flaccid, damp with the whiskey he had consumed.

"Huh?" he grunted stupidly.

Pryor shrugged, turned away. If Stone wished to drink himself into a stupor, that was the man's affair. He went through the hall, past the wounded young Sam Stone's room, the door of which was shut. So was the door of the room in which they had placed Jason Gray. The Rio Kid pushed the wooden latch, but the door was bolted inside.

"Who's there?" came Bridger's gruff voice.

"It's me — the Rio Kid."

Bridger opened the door. "So yuh made it back! I was gettin' snowshoes and gear ready to go after yuh."

The Rio Kid sank wearily to a bench.

"How's Gray?" he asked, glancing at the colonel who lay in his bunk, napping.

"He's better," replied Bridger. "He'll pull through now."

Gray awoke at sound of their voices.

"Rio Kid! Did you find 'em?"

He was weak, but there was color in his face. His blue eyes searched the Rio Kid's grim eyes. He could read the answer to his question in the tightness of Pryor's manner, his drawn face, and Gray sank back with a faint groan.

"We'll find 'em, Gray," said the Rio Kid quickly. "I come back to get food and help, that's all. The snow slowed me."

CHAPTER VIII

Smoke in the Sky

Jim Bridger went over and shut the door. The lean old scout had two pistols stuck in his belt, and there were a couple of loaded rifles leaning close at hand.

"What's wrong, Jim?" asked the Rio Kid curiously.

Bridger shrugged. "Nothin' to lay a finger on. It's just that that cussed Mormon and his whelps give me the creeps."

Pryor knew that Bridger was still angry because Mormons had driven him from his fort, before the Civil War.

"Most Mormons are hard-workin', loyal and decent men, Jim," he reminded. "And Stone's given us haven here."

"Yeah, I savvy, I savvy. But I like good Injuns — and Stone flogs them squaws when he's drunk. He's been drunk most of the time since yuh left. Somethin's worryin' him."

"How about Horton? What'd Stone do with him? Is he still locked up in that shack?"

"I don't think so. I ain't seen anybody go near the place. If yuh ask me, Stone must have give him what he had comin'."

"Huh! Mebbe. I'll ask him 'bout it when he's sober."

The Rio Kid knew he must sleep. Exhausted, he turned in, and did not really awaken until the following morning. A silent squaw fed him a substantial breakfast in the big, low-eaved kitchen, warm with the wood-burning stoves.

The sun was gleaming on the brilliant snow. Stone's Indians were busy around the ranch, caring for stock, doing the necessary work in maintaining such a large place. Stone came from his sleeping quarters as the Rio Kid started through the living room. He was somewhat sobered, but still under the influence.

" 'Mornin', Stone. I didn't find those folks, but we've got to do it. Bridger says Horton's gone."

The Mormon frowned. "Horton?"

"Yeah — the black-bearded skunk I turned over to you. The man who killed Bishop Watts and tried for me."

Stone shrugged. His lips were set.

"Those who kill Mormons always answer for it," he muttered, and turned away.

The Rio Kid did not press him. If Mormon justice had finished Fred Horton, then it was only what the man had deserved.

Pryor was haunted by the necessity of locating the lost wagon train. The Rio Kid and Bridger rigged big snowshoes. Stone had plenty of them, made of bent willow hoops and criss-crossed tough hide. On such shoes a man could travel miles over the deep Sierra snows.

With packs on back, Bridger and the Rio Kid started on their hunt. Mireles, who was young and easy-going, got along well enough with Peter Stone. Bridger was prejudiced, thought the Rio Kid. An older man was apt to have foibles, and not be as tolerant of another's faults as a younger one.

Stone was a heavy drinker. He was well-off, with his big outfit, master of all he surveyed, and could indulge himself as he chose.

"I figger they'd turn off northwest, rather than south, knowin' the trail down the escarpment as we do," the Rio Kid said to Bridger, as they crunched along on the snow. "They couldn't get too far in with their wagons in this snow. I got an idea on how to locate 'em, Jim."

"I hope it works," the old scout said pessimistically. "Once the big storms come, they're done for, and yuh might as well face it. It'll likely be another Donner party, Rio Kid. That was back in 'Forty-nine — bunch of greenhorns got caught in the Sierras, yuh savvy. Some of 'em went loco and started eatin' the others."

Several miles north of the Mormon's ranch, on a high ridge along which they had been traveling, the Rio Kid chopped up a dead pine tree and built a fire on a flat-topped rock at the summit. The afternoon air was clear, the whiteness gleaming in the sun. When he had a roaring fire going, the Rio Kid dumped green spruce limbs on his fire, and the damp evergreens crackled furiously, sending up clouds of steamy smoke.

Pryor and Bridger made coffee, ate a bite. They bivouacked there for the night. Until it grew dark, the Rio Kid kept searching the horizon but was disappointed.

In the morning — it was a fair day again — they pushed farther into the Sierras, skirting abysmal canyons. The view was breath-taking, the rock-bound Sierras magnificent, terrifying to the inexperienced beholder. Ledge on terraced ledge showed, great tumbled masses of rocks, and wide expanses of firs and pines.

The Rio Kid built another smoke fire. He watched the horizon for an hour. Bridger squatted by the flames, a strip of deer meat held on a forked stick to broil.

"Wonder if they got gumption enough to build a reply fire?" he grunted.

It was not until late afternoon that the Rio Kid suddenly exclaimed in delight.

"Jim! Look! Smoke over there!" In the clear air black vapor rose in the distance. "Ain't so far off, either!"

At noon the next day, the Rio Kid pushed up on his snowshoes to Al Drew, who was standing by the big wood fire he had going.

"Al! Where's the folks?"

Pryor seized Drew's reddened hand, and Al grinned as he pumped it.

"I had a hunch yuh'd make it, Rio Kid! They're down below, in the canyon."

A narrow split in the mountain showed close at hand. Drew was on the summits. He was relieved, and delighted to see Pryor.

"How about the colonel?" he asked. "Did yuh save him?"

"Yeah. He's at the Mormon's and he'll

pull through. Everybody all right here?"

"Yep, fine. We was short on food, though, and it was lucky I was up here, huntin'. That's how I happened to see yore smoke. The canyon's too deep to show our smoke, so I built my fire high."

"Let's get down to yore camp. I'm shore glad to see yuh."

By main strength Al Drew had beaten a path up through the drifts to the ridges, from which the wind had blown the snow. He led Pryor around to the lower canyon mouth and to the camp. Cheers rose from the throats of the travelers when they saw the Rio Kid. He had brought them through before, and they believed he would again save them.

Sue Gray ran to him, seized his arm, her pretty face anxious.

"Father — is he going to get well, Rio Kid?"

"He's in great shape, and waitin' for yuh, Sue."

"Oh, Rio Kid!" She began to cry, in joy.

The others crowded around him, telling their news.

"Look, Rio Kid!" Al Drew cried. "Gold! Yessir, real gold! We're goin' to get rich in the spring. And you're in on the strike."

"Yuh shore are, Rio Kid," agreed Keith.

They showed him the specks and nuggets they had discovered in the sands.

"It's gold, all right," he agreed. "But we can't worry about it now. Get ready to move. Yuh can't take anything but yoreselves, and we've got to pack up to the crest. I sent Bridger back to Stone's after sledges and men."

The Rio Kid was driven by the impelling knowledge that if the heavy snows came, none would ever reach safety.

"We'll lose all our belongin's?" asked Keith.

"Why not pack 'em in the cave, boys?" suggested Drew. "It won't take long. And how about the hosses, Rio Kid?"

"Mebbe they can foller the sledge tracks, they ain't bound to pull any loads," said Pryor. "Otherwise, we'll have to shoot 'em."

Two days later, the Rio Kid had them all at the Mormon's. Stone had furnished sledges and Indians to pull them. Women and children and those too weak to make the difficult run were transported on them.

Peter Stone had sobered up, somewhat. The Rio Kid conferred with him.

"Yuh'll have to feed these folks, Stone, and we'll have to take care of 'em for the winter."

"It'll cost money," said Stone.

There was a haunted look in the Mormon's brown eyes. His hands were shaky and he appeared to be rapidly going to pieces. Pryor wondered what ailed the big man. Perhaps it was the liquor that had finally weakened him.

"I got money, and we'll pay yuh," he told the Mormon. "Yuh ain't got room for so many in here. S'pose we fix up one of yore barns — that big one ought to do. They can live in there."

Stone nodded. "Suit yoreself, Rio Kid." The Mormon seemed subdued, apprehensive. He kept rubbing one fat hand over the other, licking at his thick lips.

"What's wrong, Stone?" the Rio Kid asked. "Anything I can do to help yuh?"

"Wrong? Nothin's wrong."

The people were crowded into Stone's living room, warming themselves at the two fireplaces, hungrily eating the hot food brought them by Stone's squaws.

The Mormon walked slowly among them, the Rio Kid at his side. Pryor introduced them to the man. When he had nodded to them all, he turned away.

Then Sue Gray came into the room. She had been with her father, and her eyes sparkled with happiness, the color glowed in her pretty face.

Peter Stone stopped, staring at the beautiful girl.

"Who's this, Rio Kid?" he demanded.

"Sue," said Pryor, "meet Peter Stone. This is his place, and he's goin' to take care of us through the winter."

She smiled dazzlingly. The Mormon took her hand, and held it. He could not look away from her. She wore her dark dress and a blue waist, with a knit jacket over it. Boots were on her small feet, and a pendant she had made of a light-blue pebble she had picked up hung at her throat.

"That's mighty purty," said Stone. "Where'd yuh get it, Miss Sue?"

She told him. "I have a box of them, Mr. Stone. Would you like to see them?"

"Yes'm. I collect rocks some myself. Look over here. I got a shelf filled with 'em."

The gold was kept a secret, by agreement. In the spring they would return to Lost Canyon.

They had hardly finished sheathing the barn and installed wood stoves lent them by Stone, when the heavy snows came. It was a real blizzard, with the icy wind shrieking through the Sierras. The snow fell for a week without pause, drifts twenty to thirty feet high piling up.

But the people of the wagon train were safe, snatched from an awful death by the hands of the Rio Kid.

CHAPTER IX

Gold

Winter passed and the warmth of the spring sun melted the snow from the lower Sierras. On the peaks, the snow still glistened in the brilliant light.

Through the stormy months the people of the wagon train had remained at the Mormon's, resting after their ordeal, working at the many tasks needed to be done for them to exist. There was food to be obtained and dressed and cooked, clothing to be mended, or fashioned from animal skins. And on fine days the men learned to hunt game, on snowshoes, with the Rio Kid and Jim Bridger teaching them the cunning tricks of the experienced trapper.

After the great storm which blocked the Sierra passes, Peter Stone had grown more agreeable. He had furnished the wagon train folks with everything they needed. The Rio Kid had some money, and helped defray expenses. It cost a good deal to feed and equip such a large party.

They had managed to save half their draught horses. When they were ready to leave the Mormon's, Stone loaned them animals to draw their wagons from the lost canyon to California.

Colonel Jason Gray had completely recovered from his terrible wound. He, as well as the other emigrants with new strength, were eager to tackle the job of prospecting for gold in the mountain stream. They had kept their find a secret, save from the Rio Kid and Bridger. Such news, leaking out, would bring a rush of large proportions and they might lose the benefit of their discovery.

Peter Stone grew restless, thought the Rio Kid, when the mountain passes reopened. He kept guards out on the trails, and explained, when Pryor broached the subject, that it was a precaution against hostile Indians.

"Bad bunches of Snakes come through here huntin', in warm weather," declared the stout Mormon.

Stone and his three hulking sons — Hi, Vance and Sam — Sam had mended after his hunting accident — helped drive the horses over to the canyon. It was a beautiful spring afternoon when they arrived, to find their wagons dried out by the sun and uninjured, and their goods safely cached in the big cave.

The Mormon was interested in the canyon. He made no move to leave as the sun dropped and the shadows lengthened over the camp. Colonel Gray, Drew and the Rio Kid, down at the brook to fetch water — actually they had drifted off to confer — put their heads together.

"We'll hafta wait till the Stones leave, Rio Kid," said Drew. "We want to keep that gold strike to ourselves. When we've made enough we can pay Stone for his hosses, and hand you back what yuh put out for us. Yuh give Stone all yuh had."

"Forget my part of it." The Rio Kid shrugged. "It was worth it."

His eyes strayed to Sue Gray. She was busy helping the women with supper, at the outside fireplace they had built.

Stone stayed overnight. He was up early, with the camp.

"S'pose me'n the boys give yuh a hand loadin' yore wagons, Gray?" suggested the Mormon. "Then yuh can hitch up and get started for California. Won't take long.

Yuh can be on yore way before noon."

"Yuh been a big help, Stone," said the Rio Kid. They had paid for what they had used, but the Mormon's place had been a haven. "And yuh'll get yore hosses back and money for their use. Thanks a-mighty. Bridger and I'll see 'em through all right. We won't need yore help."

Stone stared at him, as he spoke. Then he nodded.

"All right, boys. We'll be shovin' off. Wish yuh luck."

To their relief, the Mormon and his sons mounted and rode away. The eager men of the party seized picks, shovels and pans, and set to work panning the gravel and sand of the rill. It ran full, roaring through the narrow canyon bottom and swinging, to disappear in the crevice with a deep-throated, steady booming.

They needed the gold, to set them up. They had spent what little they had left. They must have something to start on in California.

Next morning, while they were hard at work panning in the stream, Peter Stone and his sons suddenly reappeared.

The Rio Kid grinned, as he met the Mormon. Stone was looking past him, at the obvious gold workings. No experienced mountain man could fail to guess what they were doing with the pans, picks and shovels, and the pile of tailings.

"So yuh smelt it out, Stone!" said the Rio Kid. "Well, now yuh savvy, so yuh might as well come in for yore share. They've found some drift gold in the crik. Get a pan and start workin'."

Hi, Vance and Sam, with rifles cradled in their stalwart arms, stared at the workings. They followed their father, as the fat Mormon moved up the bank.

"Let's see what yuh got, Drew," ordered Stone. He examined Al's findings, and the little collections of several others. Then he drew a deep sigh. "That's low-grade stuff, boys. Lot of it's pyrites, fool's gold. I've seen a dozen such strikes if I've seen one, and they were all washouts. Yuh can tell this gold came from a long ways off, and the source is prob'ly buried under a million tons of mountain! Take my advice. Pack up and get on to California."

Privately, the Rio Kid thought that Stone was probably right in his estimate of the gold strike. But a few dollars in their pockets could do no harm, and they had plenty of time before going on to their final destination in the Yosemite. He did not want to discourage these folks. Hope was a

107

great tonic. And there was always a chance of hitting something big.

"We're goin' to stay for a while, Stone," said Colonel Gray. "A month or two, mebbe three if we have luck here. We need the money. You're welcome to throw in for claims, but let's keep it to ourselves. We don't want all the world in here with us."

Peter Stone shrugged. "Fools'll always be fools," he said coldly. His lips were taut and his eyes slitted. "Yuh're wastin' time. Yuh won't pay for yore trouble with that drift stuff."

He swung and walked back, followed by his sons, to pick up the horses they had left around the bend when they had come up so quietly.

"Seems het up, don't he?" remarked Jason Gray.

"He's a queer hombre," agreed the Rio Kid.

Two days later, when Al Drew, Bridger and Mireles and he went hunting — Pryor and Bridger usually brought in the game — he had put Stone out of mind.

"You don't fancy gold diggin', do yuh, Rio Kid?" said Drew, as they rode up the winding, steep trail away from Lost Canyon.

"Nope. Jim don't either. We've seen too

many men break their hearts and backs over it, Al. It ain't the sort of work I cotton to."

"Well, I'd rather be out huntin' myself —" Al began, when the Rio Kid gripped his arm, reaching over suddenly.

"Sh! Keep shut!"

Bridger was a few yards ahead. He had pulled up his yellow cayuse and uttered a faint, sibilant warning which Pryor had caught. They dismounted, and Drew followed their example as they tied bandannas around the muzzles of their horses. Mireles took the four sets of reins, drawing off into the thick manzanita bush on the mountainside.

Bridger, already creeping ahead, looked like a trained bird dog just picking up a scent. His nostrils were wide, and he was sniffing at the wind which funneled around the tall peak.

"Can I go?" asked Al, in a whisper.

"All right," replied the Rio Kid, in the same low tone. "But keep back. Don't let any stones roll under yore feet, and do as I do."

Bridger would make a few yards, then he would flatten, listen, get up and go on. He reached a mass of big brown rocks, and took up a position from which he could

look across the slanting, uneven mountainside, down into a saddle which gaped between two peaks. He signaled back to the
Rio Kid, and Pryor and Drew inched up
beside him.

"Snake Injuns," whispered Bridger. "A
big passel of 'em."

"On the warpath, too, from their paint,"
breathed the Rio Kid.

They were ready, in case the long line of
riding savages should swing their way. But
the Snakes quickly disappeared in the
wooded saddle, around the bulge of the
adjoining peak.

Retreating, for they did not wish to
shoot and draw the large war party's attention, the white men hurried back to camp.

"Have to be mighty careful while that
bunch is in the vicinity," said Bridger.
"We'll set regular guards, and hide our
smoke. No shootin' game till we're shore
they've left."

They gave the warning but nothing
could dampen the fresh enthusiasm of the
prospectors. They had worked until their
backs ached and their muscles were stiff-
ened. None had found much gold and they
were rapidly approaching the point where
the rill emerged from the beetling precipice.

Major Rex Keith went to the horses with the Rio Kid, to quiet an unruly animal. The major was an inveterate smoker. He kept his pipe, lit or cold, between his strong white teeth most of his waking hours. He would rather have tobacco than food.

He seized the beast's mane. The horse whirled and Keith jumped back, but the animal's neck knocked the pipe from his lips and a hoof crunched it against a rock. The pipe was ruined. Keith ruefully retrieved the pieces.

"Dog it," he said, "I'm out of luck now, Rio Kid, unless I can beg another."

"Wait! I think I have one for yuh."

The Rio Kid went to his saddle-bag and found the briar pipe he had picked up on the Humboldt.

Keith was delighted. "It's a nice one. Thanks a heap."

Night had come now, so the Rio Kid, who liked to sleep in the open, rolled in his blankets outside the cave, in which the women and children and most of the men spent the nights.

At dawn he was awakened by sudden, alarmed shouts from Al Drew, who was doing a tour of guard duty down the canyon, near the constricted entrance, with

Major Keith. The Rio Kid was first on his feet, guns in hand, as the blood-chilling cry of "Indians, Indians!" echoed in the narrow canyon, banging back and forth from the steep walls.

In the new gray light, Pryor saw Al Drew running toward a bunch of armed red killers, no doubt the painted Snakes they had seen not far away, and who now were pouring through the gap. The savages were brandishing carbines, bows and arrows and long scalping-knives. They had left their mustangs back out of sight.

Drew began to shoot. Arrows and bullets hunted him but he was close on the van of the Indians, a half-dozen out in front who had gathered around someone on the ground. They were kicking, slashing and striking at the victim with their rifle butts, and Pryor knew it must be Rex Keith, the faithful, middle-aged major whom everyone loved.

"Al, get off to the side, in the rocks!" bawled the Rio Kid.

But the Indians, knowing they had been seen, were howling madly.

Drew didn't hear the Rio Kid. He rushed on in a futile effort to save Keith. He closed with the half-dozen Indians, the advance scouts of the big party. They turned on him, trying to beat him down with gun barrels, or slash him with knives. The Rio Kid knew the young fellow's extraordinary strength and his heart thrilled in spite of Al's desperate position as he saw Drew lift a stalwart bronzed Snake and, using him as a weapon, flail into the others.

The Rio Kid could not fire into the churning mass of men without hitting Al Drew. And the main body of Snakes, coming up rapidly, could not shoot Drew without injuring their chiefs. The Rio Kid opened fire, rapping bullets along the front of the massed savages.

"Come on, Bridger!" he shrieked. "Come on, boys, out and at 'em!"

Jim Bridger was already rushing toward the Rio Kid, who was crouched in the side rocks, firing swiftly. Pryor didn't need to aim at the bunched foe. His bullets spattered into them, and shrieks of rage and pain rose.

Several other men were right behind Bridger. Colonel Gray, Sergeant Lang, Corporal Burns, Lieutenant Fuller, the others were rapidly getting into action.

CHAPTER X

Torture

Grimly Jim Bridger opened fire. The Rio Kid's guns, supplemented by Bridger's and Gray's, stopped the Indians in their tracks. In that constricted space, the Snakes were caught between two unscalable walls, while the defenders could hide behind handy boulders farther up the canyon.

Drew was fighting like a wild man. He was grappling with three Indians now. Two, on the outskirts of the group, ran off, dragging Keith with them. The major was evidently dead or had been knocked out, for he was as limp as a bag of meal as they pulled him to the main gang, where he was picked up and hustled out of sight in the retreat.

Drew was suddenly free, as his remaining assailants dropped the struggle and turned, running swiftly off. One lay quiet on the ground, his head doubled under him.

Al Drew stood still for only a moment. Then, with an angry roar, he started running after his enemies, his big fists clenched. He had lost his gun in the mêlée.

"Out of the way, Al!" yelled the Rio Kid. "Yuh're in the line of fire!"

Drew heard him, and slowed. He stopped running, still inside the canyon. The Snakes were gone, rushing around the bend, picking up their mustangs.

The Rio Kid ran up to Al Drew. Al was bleeding from a dozen flesh wounds. One cheek had been laid open by a knife point. He had a nasty gash over his right eye which was swelling shut. His clothing was slashed, and big scratches and cuts poured blood from his powerful muscles. He was swearing a blue streak, however. And he was mad, for the first time the Rio Kid remembered.

"Al!" cried Pryor. "You all right?"

"Yeah! But they got the major! Come on — let's catch 'em!"

A Snake chieftain lay where Al had tossed him. He had a broken neck, was dying. Down the line lay another dead one, punctured by the Rio Kid's lead. Others, hit by the flying bullets, had been picked up and carried off in Indian fashion.

Bridger and the fighting men of the party dashed up.

"Where's Rex?" cried Gray.

"They got him," growled the Rio Kid. "He's as good as dead, if he ain't already. Al, yuh made a good fight. Lucky yuh're still alive and kickin' when yuh was at such close quarters."

"Al! Al, you're hurt!" screamed Sue Gray.

"Go back, Susan — go back!" exclaimed Colonel Gray, as his daughter hurried up. "This is no place for you. They may charge again any minute!"

But the Snakes had had a stomachful of trying to get through the narrow aisle at the canyon mouth. The Rio Kid and Bridger went to the turn, and paused. Cautiously Pryor showed the top of his Stetson, and a bullet snapped at it. The enemy was hidden around the bend, and it was as dangerous for the defenders to try to get out as it was for the attackers to enter. They were penned in the canyon.

The Rio Kid and Bridger sought to draw their foes in, but the hidden Indians covering the gap refused to show themselves.

"Huh!" growled the Rio Kid. "Reckon the rear guard's holdin' while the main bunch fades away."

He heard a woman's sobbing. Mrs. Keith had come up, to learn of her husband's awful fate. Her sons were with her, young fellows dumb with grief, who sought to comfort their mother.

Al Drew was taken back to the caves. He walked, and the smile had returned to his kind face, though he was saddened at Keith's loss.

"I done all I could to save him, but he was shot up before I got there," he kept telling the Rio Kid earnestly.

Sue Gray, working steadily, washed his wounds, and bound them, to check the bleeding. None was serious, fortunately. In his terrific fight against the big savages, luck had saved him.

Lying in the cave, on his blanket, later, Drew said:

"Yuh know, Rio Kid, I believe that's the same bunch of Injuns who attacked us on the Humboldt."

"Why?"

"I seen Bad-eyes, that funny-lookin' one I told yuh about. Remember? Yuh shot his hat off. Some of the others looked familiar, too. And a couple I grappled with cussed and grunted like white men!"

"I reckon yuh're right," growled Pryor.

"They range far and wide. Might well be the same gang, out for loot and revenge for the beatin' they got. I seen Bad-eyes, too, I know the one yuh mean. I didn't get close to him on the Humboldt."

They remained alert all day. Now and then, Bridger and the Rio Kid felt out the enemy. Bullets from hidden guns covered the narrow entrance to Lost Canyon. It was death to venture through there in the daylight.

Pryor kept patrols and sentinels out all night, but they were not disturbed. The next day was fair, peaceful. And when Pryor groped for the foe at the mouth of the canyon, no lead threatened him. The Snakes had departed, in the night, and the wagon train was free.

Free to go, if they chose. But the lure of the gold they might find held them. And to leave their fortress might be fatal, if the Indians were hidden near at hand.

Rex Keith's wife watched the Rio Kid. They had all come to look upon him as endowed with such powers that he could accomplish anything. Pryor knew what Mrs. Keith must be suffering, but she had composed herself after the first shock. Still she wanted to know her husband's fate, for certain.

At last the Rio Kid went to her, spoke gently.

"Ma'am, yuh better steel yoreself. There ain't much chance he'll survive. Prob'ly he's gone by now. But I'll go and find out for yuh. There wasn't any use in tryin' last night, for we couldn't track in the dark. I'll see what I can do."

"Thank you, Rio Kid," she said gratefully.

He took Bridger, only, in his attempt to track the Snakes. It would require the most skilled of scouts to move, with the Indians no doubt watching their back trail. Mireles stayed with the people in the cavern. On foot — for horses were out of the question for this job — Bridger and Pryor started in the afternoon.

"Only real chance is if he keeps bleedin', Jim," said the Rio Kid, after they had found a small, dried speck of blood on a round stone.

It had come either from Keith or from a wounded savage, and they moved along this line, which took them around the upper flanks of the mountain and through the wooded saddle.

Bridger was a genius at such work, and the Rio Kid knew the tricks of the trade and had an aptitude for it. They traveled silently, skilfully, flitting through the shadows of the pine woods, down low a good deal of the time, one covering the other in short advances. Now and then they picked out a dark spot, blood that had dripped from someone's wound.

It was close to dark before they reached the end of the blood trail.

"Sentry ahead," signaled Bridger.

A big Snake was up a tree, watching the back track for pursuit. It took them an hour to get around the guard. But they could out-Indian the Indian at his own game, such men as Jim Bridger and the Rio Kid.

That night they lay on the edge of a small, hidden area surrounded by dense woods and great rock slides. A spring made a pool in the shadows, and there were brush shelters with piled rock wind-shields in front of them, built against the north walls of the depression.

With moccasins on their feet, and their hair bound with kerchiefs — they left their Stetsons behind — the two spies lay flat in the thick woods, watching the camp of the Snakes. They had smeared black mud on their faces and hands and wore nothing that could rattle or catch the slightest ray of light.

"This ain't a temporary camp, Jim," breathed the Rio Kid. "It's been here a long time — all winter and prob'ly longer."

"Right. It's a hideout. Say, there's some saddles and if yuh ask me, there's white men —"

"Ssh! That sentry's turnin' our way!"

A fire burned under a jutting slab of red-brown rock that broke up the smoke and confined the glow, keeping it from showing in the sky. Snakes were there, the blanketed forms of sleeping warriors. Others were eating slabs of meat cut from a butchered horse. The camp's air was subdued, mysterious.

A big Indian with a carbine in his hands had swung to peer toward the hiding place of the two scouts. Some slight noise perhaps had attracted him.

They waited, frozen, heads down so their eyes would not gleam. The cheep of night insects and birds, the faint purling of water at the spring, and an intermittent low sound that sounded like moaning, helped them.

The sentinel finally decided his ears had deceived him and moved on. Bridger and the Rio Kid inched around, getting closer and closer to the camp. They wished to see what several Indians were standing over, to the left of the fire.

"It's Keith!" whispered the Rio Kid.

The major had been staked out near the fire. His clothing had been completely torn off, and so many arrows stuck from his naked body that he looked like a long pincushion with huge feathered needles standing out in all directions.

As the two spies watched, Keith twitched an arm, and a tall Indian bent over and slashed at the dying victim with a knife. The low groaning, which they now realized came from the throat of the sufferer, checked once again.

"He's done for," breathed Bridger.

The Snakes fiendishly had kept Keith alive to torture him. He had been slashed by a hundred knives, and arrows had been shot into his limbs and the fleshly parts of his body. Purposely they had not permitted one to strike a vital spot, preserving him for the amusement of seeing him suffer.

A powerfully-built savage emerged from one of the little huts nestling against the north side of the cliff. He strode to the fire, and, attracted by the group around Keith, turned and went to them. He was wearing a brown blanket over his shoulders and his face was smeared with oily dirt and berry paints.

His hair was bound by a wide band of rattlesnake skin.

He paused, staring down at the horrible, twitching thing that had been a man. Another Indian was squatted by the major's head, sticking his knife point an inch or so into Keith's cheeks and eye sockets.

"Calm down, Horton," said the fellow who had come out of the hut. "Yuh had enough for the night. That hombre's dead. He can't feel nothin' now."

"Reckon yuh're right, Sam," growled the other man, getting up. "I hate every man in that bunch. I only wish it was the Rio Kid and Al Drew staked out here." He ground his teeth as he wiped his long knife blade on his buckskin pants.

"Bridger, that's Fred Horton and Sam Stone!"

The Rio Kid was so startled that he nearly gave their presence away. Bridger gripped his arm with his long fingers to steady him.

"Yuh'll soon get yore chance at the Rio Kid, Drew, and the whole passel of 'em," they heard Sam Stone say to Horton. "They ain't got much ammunition left."

There was a sudden alert. A night owl called from the other side of the camp. Bridger and the Rio Kid had come in that way. Savages were awakening, seizing the rifles they slept on. But as a man rode in on a hairy little mustang, he was passed as a friend, and came over to the chiefs at the fire.

He dismounted and as he swung to Horton and Sam Stone, they could see his queer black eyes, glistening intently. One was crossed. He was chunky, ugly.

"Bad-eyes!" thought the Rio Kid. "This is the bunch that attacked the folks on the Humboldt. Now I wonder . . . well, cuss my own hide for not thinkin' of it sooner!"

He recalled how, when he had taken the wounded Jason Gray to the home of Peter Stone, that Sam Stone had been suffering from a gunshot wound. He had received it "hunting," they had explained.

And Horton, supposed to have been executed for murder by the Mormons, was here, alive and well and hand in glove with Stone's sons! Horton had shaved off his black beard. His face was smeared and he was disguised as a Snake, just as young Stone was.

Bad-eyes came close to Sam. He placed his hand, palm out, against his breast and moved it toward young Stone, who returned the salute.

"Recognition signal," decided the Rio

Kid.

Drew had described that, too. Bad-eyes had tried it on the wagon train people. When they had failed to return it, he had known they were not friends of his evil masters.

"Wonder how much Peter Stone savvies of what his boys are up to?" Pryor thought, icy fury in his heart.

Many isolated bits of a puzzle that he had hardly recognized as such were magically moving into place, forming a horrible picture.

Bad-eyes was making a report in broken English.

"Dey still dere, Chief. No mak' move, no go. Stay in canyon."

"Then they'll stay there forever," growled Sam Stone. "They should have left while they had the chance."

"We can't take any gamble on lettin' 'em go now," said Fred Horton. "They'd report and posses'd come over from California and horn in on us." The prospect of destroying the people who had saved him from death on the Humboldt Trail seemed to please Horton. "We'll shoot 'em all, except the girl. The Snakes'll enjoy the job."

"Toss yuh for that little Gray girl," said

Sam Stone.

"I've aready claimed her, Sam," snapped Horton.

The two stared at one another for a moment. Then Sam Stone grinned, shrugged, and turned away.

"One squaw's the same as another," he remarked.

He took a pipe from his pocket and filled it with tobacco from his sack, lighted up.

"I'm glad I got my good pipe back," the Rio Kid heard him say. "Keith picked it up back there when I got shot. Say, Horton, you can have the girl, but the Rio Kid and Bridger belong to me'n Hi and Vance. I shore suffered with that slug they put in me, and I always pay back what I owe."

Another man came from the shack in which Sam Stone had been.

"Come on and turn in, Sam," he grumbled. "Time yuh got some shut-eye."

"All right, Hi," Sam said, and turned back toward the shack.

CHAPTER XI

Siege

Rex Keith was no longer moaning. The two watching scouts could see the dark holes, the sockets where his eyes had been. The arrows stuck from his flesh and he did not twitch any more. Death had come, mercifully. It had been too late to save him, when Bridger and the Rio Kid had arrived.

Save for the sentinels about the camp and out along the trail, the rest went back to their blankets. The Stone boys and Horton went into the huts to sleep.

The Rio Kid and Bridger started their careful retreat, climbed a rock slide at the deep end of the vale, and headed back for Lost Canyon. They knew where the sentries were on the path, and stayed in the pine woods, sliding along like shadows.

Well out of the way, Pryor growled:

"How'd yuh like that, Jim? Stone's sons

127

were in that raidin' party way over on the Humboldt. The Snakes work for 'em, through Bad-eyes. Fred Horton, instead of havin' been killed for the death of Bishop Orson Watts, is in cahoots with the boys! Pards with 'em."

There were parts of the riddle that as yet did not fit in. He wanted more time, more information to solve it. He recalled how Peter Stone had said that men who killed Mormons must pay, and he had given Stone the clinching evidence against Horton — Bishop Watts' watch and his report book.

"Pages were torn out," he murmured.

"Huh?" asked Bridger. "What pages?"

"Pages from Watts' notebook were torn out after Peter Stone's name. What you reckon that meant? And Horton was headin' for Stone's after he tried to drygulch me!"

"What of it?" Bridger shrugged. "I told yuh that Mormon and his whelps give me the creeps."

"The Stones bein' outlaws don't make all Mormons bad, Jim," said the Rio Kid. "And after all, Peter Stone did save our friends last winter."

"It was his ranch saved us and we paid him more'n his help was worth, far as food and goods went. I'll give yuh a hunderd to one Peter Stone's in thicker'n the rest of 'em, if that could be."

"Huh. I won't take that bet. But I mean to make dead shore before strikin'. After all, them boys of his may have gone wild, and their father mightn't savvy. They could've let Horton go, and told Peter they'd finished him off."

"Yuh're an all-fired believer in the good in folks, ain't yuh?" Bridger said with a grin.

"I'm goin' to have it out with Stone himself, soon as I can," the Rio Kid told him.

They were back at Lost Canyon just before the new dawn, and Colonel Gray, in charge of the night guards, let them through.

"All's been quiet since you left, boys," reported Gray cheerfully. "I reckon we gave those savages a little too much to suit them. Bet they're a hundred miles off by now. How about Keith?"

He sobered as they told him that Keith was dead.

"I'll have to tell his wife," he said. "It's a blow."

"Keep yore sentries alert every second," ordered the Rio Kid grimly. "Them Snakes ain't as far away as yuh hope, Colonel.

They're camped not two hours' ride from here, and they got white men bossin' 'em."

"White men?"

"Yeah — Fred Horton and the Stone boys."

Gray nearly jumped out of his high soldier boots.

"Horton! I thought he was dead!"

"Me, too. But he's pinin' to nail our hides to the wall. I'd like to go over there and ambush 'em in their camp, but they outnumber us five to one and we ain't got more'n ten rounds of ammunition per man."

Bridger winked. "Yuh savvy who fixed that for us, Rio Kid," he said. "These folks never had much and they shot most of it away on the Humboldt in that battle. And remember, Peter Stone said he was too short to let 'em have any?"

"Quit harpin' on that, Jim. I admit Stone fooled me some. His ranch come in so handy, and he acted so all-fired nice when we first went there, that he blinded me. Besides, we had to use his place to save these people."

Bridger slapped him on the back, smiling. "I was only jokin' yuh, boy. Yuh're the best man I ever traveled the trail with. Anybody would have been fooled by Stone.

130

I didn't savvy what he was up to, but I shore had a funny feelin' in my old bones and I figgered it was mebbe that I didn't fancy Mormons."

The Rio Kid was worn out, in need of rest and sleep, and so was Jim Bridger. They turned in and did not awaken until suppertime. Then they got up, washed in the stream, and ate gratefully of the warm meal Sue Gray and the other women had fixed.

Al Drew was out of bed. He smiled cheerfully at Bob Pryor. He was lame and stiff from the terrific fight he had been in, but he had a grizzly bear's strength and fine recuperative powers.

Sue Gray waited on the Rio Kid. Her eyes sought his, and she was quick to smile at him.

Later he was sitting on a flat rock, outside the cavern, in the dying light when Sue came out and sat down beside him. The others were inside, talking, and resting after the day's work.

"Rio Kid," she began softly, "there's no way to thank you." There was shining gratitude in her eyes. "How could I ever repay you for saving my father, for saving all of us? Only I've got to try to tell you how I feel."

She had brought out a small leather bag with her, and she set it on the rock. Pryor took her hand, under her spell.

"You're as beautiful a girl as I ever saw, Sue," he said, "and you have wonderful spirit, as fine as anyone I ever knew."

"Thank you, Bob." There was a child-like, implicit trust in Sue's manner with the Rio Kid. "I've made this for you," she went on. "Oh, it's only colored pebbles, but it's the best I could do. I want you to take it and keep it. Some day you'll have a sweetheart and you can give it to her. Will you? For my sake?" Her smile told him how much she admired him, though, of course, she did not love him as a girl loves the man she has chosen as her mate.

"Why, she thinks I'm sort of a little tin god," he thought. It amused him, but it was ironical, too.

"Al and I are going to be married in California," Sue went on. "You helped him the other day, when he had the fight. He says they would have killed him if you hadn't been right there, shooting, and driven them off. Here's what I made for you."

She opened the bag, and took out a pendant of colored stones. They were of different hues, and their depths caught the light in a fascinating manner. She had skillfully fashioned them so they hung in a triangular form from a thin gold chain.

"I learned how to bore glass and pebbles back home in Pennsylvania, Rio Kid. You know I'm going to have a little store in California, and make pretty things. I've saved stones all the way across the Continent. I had the chain. You'll keep it, won't you, and then you can give it to *her*."

"Thank you, Sue, thanks a-mighty," he said gently.

He patted her hand, smiled, then his lonely soul drew back into itself. He took the pendant she had made and placed it in the deep pocket of his shirt and buttoned it in.

"I'll keep it over my heart," he said, patting it.

It pleased her to have given him the present. He had been thinking, before she had come to him, thinking the problem out. Perhaps the Snakes and the Stone boys wanted the wagons and goods. They were of value. Then there was the gold angle. Was it, after all, a valuable strike that they had come upon, and was the enemy after the metal?

After dark, he sought out Bridger and Gray.

"I'm goin' over to Stone's," he said. "I'll go alone. Jim, you stick here with Mireles and the rest and make shore yuh hold off them Snakes. I got to have it out with Peter Stone. And then, mebbe I can pick up some help on the trail. Parties ought to be comin' through now. The road's passable."

He saddled the dun, Saber, and took his leave by way of the guarded bottleneck. There was a half moon, and the way was light enough for riding. Wind moaned in the Sierra peaks, and the mountains stood out black against the sky. He kept a hand on his Colt, ready for trouble, but he was not stopped. Close to dawn he reached the trail to the Mormon's.

The stars had paled, the sky showed blue and the world was bathed in gray light when he came out of the evergreens and swung Saber toward the big ranch. And suddenly he pulled up, with a stifled curse.

Where Pete Stone's had stood, there was nothing. No buildings were there, nestling against the cliff, or in the open. The big barn in which the wagon train folks had wintered was gone, as were the stables, the corn-cribs, the little lock-up from which Fred Horton had escaped. Nothing remained.

As he rode closer, he saw that the whole great area of the vale, cleared by Indian hand labor, was black. Where the house and other structures had stood were charred heaps of carbon, ugly masses of burnt desolation. The grass and near-by trees had been burned as the fire had spread, but the woods had been damp from spring rains and, after its first savage rush, the fire had stopped and died out on the wet edges.

The Rio Kid sat Saber, staring, hunting for some sign of life about the Mormon's. It had been a busy place, with Indians and cattle, horses and other animals around. Now it was utterly deserted. A brooding, desolate air, like death, hung over the clearing.

The startled Rio Kid could scarcely credit his eyes. He stayed where he was, just watching, but nothing moved.

After a time he slowly turned the dun. Then the wind, from the east, brought him the click of shod hoofs on the rocky up-trail, and he quickly drew back into the bush and rocks at the side of the Sierra road.

"Mebbe it's somebody can tell me what hit the Mormon's," he thought as he waited, concealed as a precaution.

Four men came along, on sweated horses. They were white men, and in the lead was a masterful rider, a man in blue with a massive, handsome head, a thick walrus mustache, and luxuriant curly hair under his cocked dark Stetson. His nose was large, and his darting eyes were deep-set.

The riders with him wore corduroy and high-laced boots, brown Stetsons with sunbrims. But though they were younger than the leader they were puffing and looked jaded, evidently hard put to it to keep up with him.

"General — General Dodge!" called the Rio Kid, pushing out.

General Grenville Dodge reined in his big horse, swinging to face the Rio Kid. His face wreathed in smiles and he returned the Rio Kid's snappy military salute.

"Captain Pryor! Mighty glad to see you. I was getting worried about you. Where's Bridger?"

"He's safe. At least he was when I left him a few hours back, General. We made the survey for yuh. It's as Bridger showed yuh on the maps, and I agree with him. You'll have to run along the Humboldt or close to it for three hundred miles or so. Utah route joins in with it."

"These boys are engineers, Pryor," Dodge said, and named his companions swiftly.

They were glad of the chance for a rest, to get down, stretch, and roll cigarettes, drink from their canteens, then sit on flat rocks along the trail. The far bank was cut into a reddish clay bluff. Behind the Rio Kid were thick pine woods, and more on the higher side.

"We're going to stop at Stone's for dinner," went on Dodge. He was a dynamic, dominant character.

"Yuh won't get no dinner there," drawled the Rio Kid, "unless yuh like charcoal, General. It's burnt to the ground."

He gave Dodge a quick recital of what he had found.

"We run into this wagon train, under attack on the Humboldt," he explained. "Snakes, we figgered, though we decided there were a few whites disguised, mebbe. We managed to get 'em to Stone's for the winter, then they went back to a canyon where they'd been lost in the snow. Same gang attacked again — and this time Bridger and I proved it. Stone's sons and a killer named Fred Horton are leadin' the Injuns, and they mean to destroy us and our wagon train friends."

Dodge frowned as he pulled at his thick mustache.

The man knew the West, though he was

a native of Massachusetts. He had studied engineering, and when the Civil War broke out, he had entered the Army and rapidly advanced to the rank of general officer. He had fought the Indians in 1866, and had been chosen Chief Engineer of the Union Pacific Railroad.

For the job he needed all the terrific driving force of his dominant nature, since there were thousands of problems to be solved. But he had not considered it necessary, in making this trip for the railroad, to be surrounded by fighting men.

"I have only these boys with me, Rio Kid," he said, "and you need real help against such a large force of Indians. I'll hustle through to Sacramento, and we'll hope to get a posse back in time to aid you. Draw me a sketch of the position where your friends are under siege, so we can find you.

"I'm on my way to confer with Stanford and other Central Pacific men, but am coming straight back once our business is settled. That won't take long, and I'll start the relief force as soon as I arrive. No doubt I'll overtake it before they reach you."

CHAPTER XII

Death in the Night

During the Civil War the Rio Kid had learned field sketching. Such maps, showing the position of enemy forces and fortifications, were a vital branch of the soldier's training.

"Don't know as I've got a pencil and paper," he said to General Dodge, in answer to the suggestion the railroad man had made.

He felt in his pockets. A sudden idea occurred to him, and he drew forth the pendant which Sue Gray had given him.

"That's pretty!" exclaimed Dodge, as the light caught its colors.

One of his engineers furnished the Rio Kid with pencil and paper and Pryor quickly indicated the position of Lost Canyon.

"I'm goin' back, General," he said then.

"I'll see yuh if we're still kickin'. . . . Will yuh do somethin' for me in California?"

"Anything I can," the general said promptly.

The Rio Kid told him, quickly, what he wanted done.

As they were shaking hands, the Rio Kid's eyes lifted over Dodge's sturdy, massive head, staring beyond the man.

"What's wrong?" inquired the general.

Pryor didn't immediately answer. The wound in his side, where the flesh had healed unevenly, kept itching.

"I don't know," he said, in a low voice. "But I got a feelin' we're bein' watched."

He had had it, all along, ever since he had reached the desolated spot where the Mormon's had stood. It was an uncomfortable sensation that kept forcing him to look around, to drop a hand to his Colt.

He dismounted, and went up to the clay bank, gun in hand, ready for trouble. Dodge and his men covered him.

Thick bush and the long-needled pines faced him in a blank wall. No sounds betrayed the presence of a hidden enemy. He crouched, pushing through the grasping pine branches. He saw nothing, heard nothing except the noises of birds and squirrels, the faint sough of the breeze in the tree-tops.

Then his trained eye suddenly caught a slight movement of a tiny sprout, a sassafras bush sending up its first greenish shoot. It was near the edge of the woods, so that the sunlight could enter and spot it. It was half bent, but it was gradually straightening, a slow motion as the sprout returned to upright.

He moved to it. The bark at the base was freshly cracked. The brown needles and leaves, blown here or dropped, seemed more firmly pressed down for about five or six feet — the length of a man's prostrate body.

"Somebody was lyin' there, listenin'!" he decided.

He gripped his Colt and pushed farther in. But there was nothing in the dense woods to draw him. No shot, no sounds save Nature's.

Cold prickles were on his flesh. He was not afraid of anything, but he liked to see his opponent. It was baffling, too, such a sensation. He felt he was being watched, and yet he could not surprise the spying beings who dogged him.

After a quick search which yielded nothing he returned to Dodge, who was impatient to get along.

Saying good-by, the Rio Kid watched the party start up the slope to the summits. Turning then, he shoved Saber into the woods, heading for Lost Canyon.

He had gone about a mile, and had come out on the trail through the Sierras, winding up and down, and along the ridges toward the camp, when the uneasy sensation of being followed, dogged, again overwhelmed his trained senses.

On the next height he left his horse and climbed a noble tall pine, the sticky resin gumming his fingers. He could see back over the woods. Some small specks in the sky moved, flying off in two directions, as though alarmed.

"Huh! Somebody is trailin' me!"

Determined to catch whoever it was, he went down, and rode on for a time. Then he drew off the trail, and hid his horse and himself in a thicket.

He waited, half an hour, an hour. Nothing.

Swearing to himself, he knew he must move on. He was anxious about his friends, aware that Horton and the Snakes would again attack, try to destroy them. Dodge would send help if he could raise it in time, but the Rio Kid wanted to be in for the fight. The wagon train folks did not have much ammunition, and if the Stone boys and Horton drove the Indians to a determined rush, sacrificing enough men in the first rushes, they would force the party to expend their ammunition entirely, and thus be at the mercy of the attackers.

"If we have to, we can all hide in the cave," the Rio Kid thought. "They'll get our hosses and wagons, but they'll have to come right up on our guns to kill us."

It would be a last resort, that. He did not like to give up the canyon, for they would be unable to get fresh water from the brook, and they would lose their animals.

He mounted Saber, half expecting to be fired upon. Whoever was trailing him was fiendishly skilled at the job. If he had had the time, he might have outwaited or doubled back, to ambush the skulking tracker, but the sense of urgency as to the fate of the people ahead drove him on.

"Cuss yuh, foller if you want," he growled, shaking a fist at the silent, deserted back trail.

Later, with the spring sun hot at his left, he heard the sound of gunfire. It came from Lost Canyon. He pushed closer. At a safe distance, he turned Saber loose, aware that he must go the rest of the way afoot.

"Keep away, boy, and I'll call you when I want yuh," he told the dun, who nuzzled his hand, and sniffed. He understood.

Pryor cached his saddle, and let Saber run free. The horse would wait for him, would come when he called.

Carbine in hand, and guns strapped on, he took to the woods, off the beaten trail to Lost Canyon.

Off to the south, he crept to a ridge crest, and peered over. He could see the Snakes in the narrowing entry of Lost Canyon, big bronzed figures. The siege was on again.

"Have to wait till dark," the Rio Kid muttered. "Then I'll get through one way or another."

The Indians were there in force. The Rio Kid could no longer worry about whoever had been after him on the way over from the site of the Mormon's. He yearned to be in there, fighting to help his friends hold off the Snakes. There were well over a hundred hard-fighting braves in the gang, officered by Stone's sons and the vicious Fred Horton.

"Wonder where Peter Stone is," he thought. "He might have been sleepin' in one of them huts at the hideout. On the other hand, mebbe his boys have run hog-wild on him."

Great bands of mustangs were being carefully guarded by sentries, back from the battlefield. The Snakes and their white leaders had made a bivouac in a patch of red pines to the right of Lost Canyon entry. From his eyrie, the spying Rio Kid could see a dump of bags and gear, no doubt ammunition with which to replenish the stores they carried on their persons; and food supplies.

"Wish I could get to that," he muttered.

He watched through the next two hours. There were always several men around the ammunition dump, and it was to one side, close to a group of blanketed figures sheltered behind some rocks. Apparently they were the chiefs, for messengers came out of the narrow canyon mouth to report, and returned with orders to the fighters.

The cooling spring wind off the Sierras brought him bursts of gunfire from time to time. "At least the folks are still fightin'," he thought.

He was impatiently awaiting the darkness. He knew of but one way to enter Lost Canyon and that was through the constricted defile. This would mean passing through the heart of the enemy.

The sun, ruby red, dropped swiftly behind the peaks and the sky was a gorgeous display of purples, golds and blues when he prepared to make a move. He had spied out the positions of sentries guarding the rear and flanks of approach to the enemy camp, and as soon as dark came he began his dangerous game. He had left his riding boots with his saddle and donned his moccasins. His guns were stuck in his soft leather belt, with his knife, so that no leather might creak — the usual precautions.

While it was light he had chosen his spot — the end of a sentry's beat. The night was now upon the Sierras and the wind chilling. The shooting inside Lost Canyon had slacked off but occasionally he heard the snap of a carbine.

The rocks and the patches of pine, spruce and smaller growth were rustling, sinister black blotches in the night. Using all his skill, the Rio Kid spent over an hour getting into position. At last he was lying flat on his chest, head down, only a yard off the faint trail. The sentry was passing him, and Pryor could hear the Indian's breathing.

Against the slight glow from a sheltered fire in the enemy camp, he could, for an instant, see the flitting, silent figure of the blanketed Snake. It was cold in the mountains. The Indians wore buckskin pants, and at night heavy blankets sometimes lined with animal fur.

The man he had marked was tall and sinewy. He carried a short-barreled carbine in his right hand, and belted about his lean waist were ammunition containers and his scalping-knife. As he turned and started back, his eyes reflected the red fire glow. He was sniffing the wind with its tang of burning pine wood mingled with the delicious odors of broiling beef slabs and coffee. Horton and the Stone boys had come prepared to be comfortable.

The Snake Indian paused with his legs within arm's reach of the invisible Rio Kid, whose hands and face were stained black. Then he moved on. As he turned, facing the light of the camp, the Rio Kid sprang.

He had one chance and no more to succeed in silencing the sentry. A slight error and the Indian would have cried out, given the alarm, and spoiled the plan. But the steel muscles of Bob Pryor's left arm vised across the Snake's lean throat from behind, as a knee rammed into the small of the Indian's back. An instant later his knife drove into the red man's vitals, and the killer was done.

Two minutes later, a sentry walked with gliding gait on along the trail, blanket high around his blackened cheeks. It was the Rio Kid, who had taken the place of the Snake on duty. He walked boldly out into the light, passed another guard off to the right, and turned past the headquarters camp.

There were a good many Indians near the fire, warming themselves, or eating. A group of half a dozen squatted on the other side of the coals. One was Bad-eyes, and the Rio Kid, his head down, saw stalwart, blanketed forms with stained faces that he guessed must be Horton and the Stone boys. A snatch of lingo reached him — the harsh tones of tough whites over the murmur of the Indian braves.

He slouched on past, to the canyon entrance. Someone sang out to him but he waved the carbine taken from the Snake and they did not follow him. There was an armed man leaning against the rock wall on his left as he passed through the narrows, but the Rio Kid grunted and kept going.

Vague figures showed up the canyon. A rifle banged and he glimpsed the flaming of the shot. He stayed on the stream bank. There were snipers and watchers lying in cover behind rocks and the sandbanks.

"They've got 'em holed up in the cave!" he thought.

He could see the black bulks of the big prairie schooners, but the horses of the emigrants had been driven off by the Indians. It must have been a desperate battle, for Bridger to have allowed them to breach the pass into the canyon.

The ticklish task of getting in with the beseiged whites without having them shoot him down faced the Rio Kid. A Snake called to him from nearby rocks, in the Indian tongue. He only waved his gun. The Indian did not shoot. That there were whites allied with the savages was the Rio Kid's good fortune.

He edged closer to the cavern mouth. It was a black slit against the dark of the cliff, and utterly silent.

Suddenly he saw a gun flame, pointed toward him. The bullet missed him by hardly an inch.

"Bridger — Drew!" he shouted, putting down his head to run. "It's the Rio Kid! Don't shoot!"

CHAPTER XIII

Captured

Sentinels below were too late in realizing the trick of the Rio Kid. They could not spot him against the black wall. Futile slugs whirled by him, and he called again, to his friends.

He had only about twenty-five yards to cover, before he dived into the cavern mouth. Bridger had him by the arm in a moment.

"Rio Kid! By glory, somethin' shook my hand just as I let go! I was aimin' for you — thought yuh was a Snake creepin' up!"

The Rio Kid was panting, but quickly regained his breath. Bridger had Al Drew, Sergeant Lang, Mike Reilly and a couple of younger boys, Major Keith's sons, on the line at the mouth of the cavern. They had piled up large rocks for a breastworks, and scooped out holes behind them in the loose, sandy floor.

"I seen General Dodge," said the Rio Kid. "He'll send help to us soon as possible. We'll have to hold 'em off till then — mebbe three, four days."

Bridger chuckled. "I told yuh yuh was a wishful cuss, Rio Kid! They charged us this afternoon and drove us inside. Got the hosses and wounded Corporal Burns and Bill Keith — not bad, though. They're only pinks."

"How much ammunition did yuh shoot off, Jim?" asked the Rio Kid.

"Seven rounds per man. We got about three left, I'd say, countin' duds. It was tough-and-go for a half-hour there. One more run like it and we'll be done."

Bridger shrugged. The old scout was not afraid. He had been through too many dangerous situations to know the meaning of fear. He was only stating cold facts.

Back in the recesses of the main cavern were the women and children and the rest of the party. Bridger left Al Drew in charge of the guards, and went back a short distance with the Rio Kid.

"They'll charge us from the sides tomorrer, at dawn," he said in a low voice. "I been in too many of these scraps not to savvy what an enemy'll do next. We can pick off thirty, even fifty, but then we're finished."

The Rio Kid knew Bridger's keen senses too well to doubt it. What Bridger said the attackers would do would be the logical tactics, since they knew how short of ammunition the wagon folks were.

"Give me a drink, will you, Jim?" the Rio Kid said. "I run like a locoed steer gettin' in here."

Bridger cleared his throat. He seemed embarrassed.

"We ain't got any water," he finally said. "Blame me if yuh want. I should have had some in here, but I was catnappin' when they charged this afternoon. I been meanin' to go down into them lower caverns in back. I can smell water, and there may be some there. So far we ain't suffered and I been mighty busy keepin' them Snakes out of here."

"I'll take a look-see," said the Rio Kid. "There may be pools back there, Jim. Where's Mireles?"

"Restin', after the fight this afternoon."

Celestino had heard his partner's low voice. The Mexican came to his friend and touched his hand. His white teeth gleamed in a smile of welcome relief.

"General! I feel you were near! *Si*."

The situation was as desperate as it could get, without actual surrender to the murderous enemy. They would draw the last slugs of the defenders, and then the Snakes would be on them with their knives and arrows. There could be no mercy, and the Rio Kid did not for a moment even consider that. The Stone boys, Horton, and Bad-eyes, would kill them all by torture, except the younger women and the girls.

"I'd sort of hoped they'd wait a few days, and give Dodge time to reach us with help," murmured the Rio Kid. "But he'll never make it now, Jim. What's yore idea?"

"Shucks! Fight to the last drop of the hat. We'll get back in there like so many wildcats and they'll pay to pull us out. We'll kill the women first, though. I'm in favor of usin' our last bullets for 'em. It's better, and a man fights to the end a lot happier than if he's worried about his wife and daughters."

"Wish I could get my paws on some of that ammunition they got stored outside the canyon," growled the Rio Kid. "They got it close guarded, though. And I couldn't work that trick again, from this direction. . . . Well — I'm goin' down and see if I can find some water below, Jim. Want to come?"

"Me, too, General," said Mireles.

The three went past the huddled figures of the party. Some were sleeping, but others lay tense, waiting. The imagination of men quailed at the thought of what savages could do to a sensitive human body, of the cruelties their loved ones would suffer.

"Must be more to this than just revenge and the wagons, Jim," said the Rio Kid, as they moved slowly in the lower recesses of the caverns.

Mireles had lighted a pine torch, from a pile which lay near the wall. Al Drew had placed them there for Sue, so that the girl could hunt the colored stones she loved.

"Mebbe they want the gold," grunted Bridger. "Though there's ain't been much of a strike here."

The cave grew narrow and rather close. The walls of clay were damp, and here and there they saw a colored rock sticking from the sides.

"If there's any water, it's over this way," said Bridger, swinging left. "Looks to me like that stream used to run through here at one time, Rio Kid. Then it lowered its bed and drove through below, where it runs now."

"Yuh're right, Jim. Water does funny things, don't it?"

He stopped, raising the smoky torch so that its light showed the reddish rocks which apparently blocked them from going further. He listened. There was a dull, steady sound.

"I hear water runnin', boys. Must be a crack round here somewheres."

He tried the right side of the big rocks, found a black gap hidden from the front, which he was able to squeeze through, head-first, the torch held out before him. The lean Bridger and Mireles followed, and they could stand up in a V-like cavern which adjoined the other.

Moving on, the new passage widened out in a series of underground chambers.

"Look at them colored rocks!" exclaimed Bridger. The light glinted from the clay walls.

"Water ain't far ahead!" said the Rio Kid.

The beating of the stream echoed louder, with a hollow sound in the high-roofed cave. They pushed on, and reached the ditch of rock which the rill had cut for itself through the mountain.

"This is it!" said the Rio Kid. "The

brook comes this way!"

He lay down to drink in the stream that disappeared in blackness to the right. On the left were crevices, splits in the solid rock of the mountain, through which it came in.

Getting up, he lighted another torch from the dying one. A ledge ran along the torrent. He started to walk it, driven by curiosity and a sudden hunch, hardly more than a vague hope. For several hundred yards they moved with the water, the tunnel getting narrower and narrower. Then they reached the end, a hole into which the underground brook dropped with a dashing, gushing beat.

He held out the torch, trying to see how deep the hole might be. A gust of wind puffed the light out and they stood in pitch darkness.

"Light a match, Celestino," ordered Bridger.

The Mexican was feeling in his pocket for a match. The Rio Kid stood there, sniffing. Water made currents in the air as it moved, but he scented something else.

"Hold it!" he commanded. "Let our eyes get used to the dark, boys."

They waited. The Rio Kid looked up.

His eye pupils accustomed to the blackness, he saw a single star high in the heavens.

"Light up and give me a boost!" he ordered. "There's a crack through to the side of the mountain!"

The Rio Kid squeezed his lithe body through the crevice. There were thick bushes surrounding the layered outcroppings of rock on the steep east slope. The enemy camp lay below, to his left, and he could not see the canyon for he had come through the underground tunnel and emerged on the far shoulder of the huge split mountain.

Bridger and Celestino were still in there. He kneeled, calling in a low voice:

"Wait for me, boys. I'll take a look-see."

A cold wind cut him as he crawled from the swale of underbrush and broken rock. There was a pine woods lower down and he entered it, creeping on. It was black under the canopy of spreading branches but it was also relatively easy to move with fair speed. He felt his way, pausing often to listen and to peer ahead.

He stopped again, came up on his knees so he might pick a further route. The old wound in his side itched frantically.

He was hit violently from the rear and both sides. Before he could get at his guns or knife, black shapes rose thick about him and he was knocked flat under a crushing weight of bodies. He tried to fight, sure that the Snakes had him, but his breath was driven from him as knees jolted into the small of his back. He was held to the mat of pine needles, which stabbed at his cheeks and eyes.

They jerked his arms painfully up behind him and tied his wrists and his ankles. He was roughly rolled over and a smelly hand covered his mouth.

Breathless, he tried to identify his captors, but they were vague shadows, black save for the faint animal shine of eyes watching him through slits in black cloth hoods. In the second he could think he realized they were not Indians.

No one said anything. They gathered about him, and he sensed from the rustle that there were a great many of them. The hand on his lips relaxed.

"What yuh goin' to do with me?" he said, and the hand stopped his mouth again.

Soft sounds of approach, and more men came up. One, evidently a chief, pushed through and squatted by him, a giant black shadow. The hand was taken from his lips.

"Yore name?" demanded a gruff voice. "Keep yore voice down or we'll cut out yore heart."

"I'm the Rio Kid. Who are you?"

"We ask the questions, we don't answer 'em."

Another came in, from one side, a man who evidently had been sent for.

"He says he's the Rio Kid," reported Bob Pryor's questioner. "We don't want no witnesses. Better finish him off."

"Reckon yuh're right," said the burly, stocky chief who had been called. The voice was cool, and noncommittal, but it was decisive, too. There was no touch of pity in it.

The Rio Kid suddenly had the answer.

"Hickman!" he gasped. "Bill Hickman! So yuh're Mormon Avengin' Angels!"

"He savvies us, see?" snapped Hickman's lieutenant. "Bill, dead witnesses can't squawk. Mountain Meadows done ruined us and we can't afford any more stories agin the Saints. Brigham wouldn't like it."

The Rio Kid knew Bill Hickman's character, knew there was no softness, no mercy in the man. On the other hand, he was shrewd and sensible. Pryor showed no alarm. He spoke easily, straight at

Hickman, who was in absolute military command of the Danites or Avenging Angels, a secret band which acted in a punitive capacity within the Mormon circle.

"I got plenty to tell yuh, Hickman. Remember how we met on the salt desert, beside Bishop Watts' remains? I can show yuh the man who killed Watts and robbed him of his hoss and valuables. I got all sort of evidence against the sons of Peter Stone, too. They're in cahoots with a big tribe of Snakes who've been attackin' wagon trains on the Humboldt!"

He kept his brain steady, calculating, feeling the way. It flew to many happenings. He remembered the burnt ranch, and how he had been watched, trailed. The Danites had burned Stone's to the ground, so they were after him.

Hickman was interested. This was his business. "Yuh mean it?" he demanded. "Who killed the Bishop?"

"An hombre named Fred Horton." The certainty of it, as he fitted the isolated bits of the deadly mystery together, gave the Rio Kid confidence. "Look, Hickman. The Bishop checked up on the stories of survivors of attacks on the trail — some must have been Mormons. White men were with the Indians, leadin' 'em; you knew that, or guessed it.

"Bishop Watts carefully checked these accounts, and wrote about 'em in his notebook. Horton got that book, along with the Bishop's pocketbook and watch. He found evidence against Peter Stone in it, tore out the pages, and headed for Stone's to warn him and throw in with him, as he did. After killin' Watts he joined a wagon train along the Humboldt, for protection and to get food and water. Then he deserted it.

"He tried to drygulch me and take my hoss. I caught him, turned him over to Peter Stone, who pretended to kill him for Watts' death, but he let him go so's Horton could fight for him. Stone savvied from what Horton told him that you was suspicious, on his trail. His sons had attacked and destroyed Mormons as well as others, robbin' for the loot and sport."

Hickman grunted. The Rio Kid knew he had it right. In his keen mind he was sorting out his clues, putting them in their rightful positions.

"Is this Fred Horton a tall, strong hombre with mebbe a black beard?" Hickman demanded.

"That's him. He's shaved off his beard now, though."

"He killed Watts, eh? He was doin' holdups of well-to-do Saints in Salt Lake City, and the police were after him. He killed one who tried to arrest him and run off. But I didn't savvy he'd done in the Bishop." Hickman was silent for a moment, and then he ordered shortly, "Let the Rio Kid loose."

Pryor's bonds were cut. He sat up, and he knew he had won.

"I savvy you, Rio Kid," said Hickman. "Yuh got a good name on the Frontier. But we got to be careful. Some folks hate the Saints and there's talk of investigations. We got to move quietlike."

It was as close to an apology as Hickman had ever come.

"We seen yuh with General Dodge, and heard some of yore talk, enough to make us foller yuh over this way, but couldn't figger what them Snakes below had to do with Stone and us, so we waited, hid up here. Reckoned they was after some prospectors in the canyon, but that wasn't our affair."

Hickman would have let the whites die, rather than interfere. They were not Mormons.

"Yuh savvy where this Horton sidewinder and the Stones are now, Rio Kid?" he asked.

"Yeah. S'pose we throw in together, Hickman, for the time bein'?"

Hickman grunted. "Yore evidence makes it easy for us. Nobody can say these hombres don't deserve what they'll get. I been feelin' around in the dark till now. Brigham ordered me to be mighty careful. When Stone run away, I figgered he must be guilty, so we . . . Well, what's yore idea?"

"Horton and the Stone boys are disguised as Snakes, Hickman. They're down below. That's their camp. Peter Stone's with 'em, or else I savvy where he's hidin', not too far from here. My friends and I'll stand up for the Mormons. Yuh'll be heroes for savin' their lives. We can hit the killers, pen 'em in the canyon, sweep up Horton and the Stones and the whole dirty kaboodle of 'em!"

"Cuss Stone!" said Hickman. "He was gettin' rich, raidin' the trails. The dirty renegade, killin' his own people, the Mormons."

On the wind, came the sudden crackling of heavy gunfire. They heard dim but shrill Indian war whoops. The Rio Kid realized that the first gray of the new dawn was in the sky.

"We got to work fast, Hickman! Here's how we'll do it. . . ."

CHAPTER XIV

All Out

Lithe Snake warriors moved in for the kill, in the misty shadows of the morning. Aware of the pitiful supply of ammunition their victims held, they were bold, showing themselves for instants as they fired, then dropping or jumping to cover, seeking to draw lead.

Heavy volleys roared from the carbines, spattering into the cave and slapping the rock barricade behind which crouched the defenders. There were whites in there, men and women who would provide great sport. There was plenty of loot in the big wagons and pay promised by their renegade chiefs, the Stones and Horton. Bad-eyes had command of the Indians, under his white leaders.

They were sure of the kill, and had orders to push it through to the ghastly, bloody climax. A few rounds, and the emigrants would be finished.

Whooping savagely, shooting a hail of bullets at the dark cave entry, they charged. There was hardly any reply as they converged, moving fast, flitting through the rocks. A bunch massed to dash in, emboldened by the lack of resistance. Bad-eyes leaped into view, carbine raised over his ugly head. He cried to them in Snake, to charge.

They rushed — and from close range a terrific volley roared, slashing them. The front rank went down, and Bad-eyes caught a slug in the nose, another in the breast. He flipped into the air, dead before he landed.

A second tearing roar of gunfire settled it for the moment. The Snakes shrieked, split up, running for cover in the rocks, or off to the sides out of range.

Big men, their disguised white leaders, hurried from the rear, from cover, beating at them with rifle barrels, cursing them.

"Go on and get 'em, cuss yuh!" howled Fred Horton, dancing up and down. "They ain't got but a few bullets left!"

Two Snakes, runners, came dashing full-tilt from the canyon entrance, shrieking to the chiefs. In the din and confusion they

165

were not heard. And the Rio Kid, with Bill Hickman at his side, took aim as he made the turn, hot on their heels.

"I got the one on the left, Rio Kid," Hickman said.

Both runners checked in their flight, rolled over and over, lay still.

The Indians and their white leaders heard the new guns. They turned, looking toward the entrance to Lost Canyon. Horsemen broke through in a long line that opened across in a skirmish formation to sweep the canyon.

Peaked black hoods covered the heads and torsos of the riders. Slanted holes gave a semblance of eyes and there were other openings for noses and mouths. Their appearance struck terror into the Snakes. Trapped in the canyon, with no way out, the Indians spread, hunting cover in the rocks. A bunch tried again to charge the cave, but were met by heavy volleys that turned them off.

With the Rio Kid and Hickman in the van, and with hand signals giving commands, the Danites expertly swept up the foe.

"There's the Stone boys, Hickman!" the Rio Kid cried. "The big ones, over at the right."

Hickman swerved his powerful black horse. He moved straight toward the armed trio. The Rio Kid was near him.

"Mormons," Hickman sang out coldly, "throw down yore guns!"

Hi, Vance and Sam Stone stood as though rooted to the spot. They knew the fate that had caught up with them. Lines of masked Danites were coming up. There was no way out. The young renegades began to tremble.

"Hickman!" one of them sobbed. "Don't — don't —"

Bill Hickman did not reply. He signaled, and some of his men seized the broken killers.

"How about Horton?" demanded Hickman, turning off with the Rio Kid. "We got the Stones, but I want Watts' killer."

A bullet that tore a jagged hole in the peak of Hickman's hood made him break off. His horse was startled, and fought at his rider.

"He's over in them rocks, Hickman!" cried the Rio Kid. "I'll toss you for who takes him!"

He was on Saber. He had picked up his mount after making his plans with Hickman. Ammunition had been passed through to Bridger and Mireles, and taken into the caves, so the besieged could hold off the charge.

The Rio Kid rode swiftly toward the jagged nest of rocks, under the steep west wall. A slug whirled past him, and he left his saddle. Hickman was a foot behind, on the other side, and they started into the rocks together, the Mormon with his carbine held short, the Rio Kid gripping a Colt.

Big boulders sheltered them save when they had to climb over the top of one, and so show themselves to Fred Horton.

The Rio Kid got there first. Horton, his eyes flaming, his stained face twisted, swore at him shrilly. Hickman was coming in from his left, and Horton fired hastily at the Rio Kid as Pryor threw himself over a high rock, and landed within a few yards of the killer.

"Cuss yuh, Rio Kid!" the man's voice broke with a craven note.

He tried again to shoot, but the Rio Kid's Colt roared. There was a slight smile on his straight lips as he let go of his hammer spur. His bullet hit Horton's forehead, drilled his brain. The powerful man collapsed, as Bill Hickman jumped in and poured bullets from his carbine into the body.

"Save yore lead, Hickman," said the Rio Kid. "I beat yuh to it."

He searched Horton's clothing, brought out Watts' gold watch.

"So that's Horton!" Hickman said grimly. "Orson Watts is avenged."

They made their way out. The Danites had picked up their prisoners, herded them together, disarmed them.

Hickman took charge of the blubbering Stone boys. They marched ahead of him, as he rode, grimly, coldly silent.

Bridger, Mireles, Al Drew and Sue, Colonel Gray and the others were emerging from their cave prison. The Rio Kid waved to them, and trailed Hickman through the gate to the camp where the Snakes and their white chiefs had bivouacked. Several Mormons in black hoods held the spot. They had a dozen prisoners herded against the wall.

A stout Indian sat on a flat rock, the picture of abject dejection. His fat hands wrung one another. He was apparently a mass of quivering flesh, and when Hickman came up he began to shake like so much jelly.

"Peter Stone," said Hickman, "yuh are under arrest. Yuh have killed yore last Mormon."

Stone's mouth hung open. He was completely unnerved. The fear of Hickman and his Avengers had sent him running from his eyrie strongholds, had driven him to desperate measures.

"What was yuh so all-fired bent on gettin' here in Lost Canyon, Stone, that yuh drove the Snakes to massacre them folks?" demanded the Rio Kid.

Stone did not even look at him. His eyes were riveted to the icy gray orbs of Hickman.

"Answer!" Hickman said.

Stone gulped. "I — I wanted the jewels."

"What jewels?" asked the amazed Rio Kid.

"Answer!" ordered Hickman.

It was as though Stone were hypnotized.

"The — the gems that girl found. There's a bushel of 'em in those caves."

"How do yuh savvy that?" asked Pryor.

Again Hickman had to tell the fat man to reply.

"I had a couple — opals, one a fire opal, another a common pearly blue one. An Indian we picked up, dyin' of a wound, told me about an underground cave full of 'em. He had a few with him. He died before he could tell just where the canyon was, but he waved this-a-way. I hunted it for two years, but never had any luck, till that Gray girl come along with a boxful. I — I wanted 'em all."

Now the Rio Kid understood the Mormon, knew why Stone had helped them, what he had hoped to gain.

"Yuh needed wealth yuh could carry when yuh run from Hickman," he growled. "Yuh had a lot of stuff yuh'd looted but yuh couldn't take it with yuh, and Hickman burned yore stores and ranch. The gems would have made yuh rich."

Stone was not interested in the Rio Kid, or in anything except the gray eyes which held him. "Get up," ordered Hickman.

The stout killer rose. His knees would hardly hold him. At Hickman's command, he walked to a saddled horse, and mounted, sagged in the leather. The Stone boys were being tied to mounts. The Danites worked purposefully, with few words.

"*Adios,* Rio Kid," said Bill Hickman. "We'll be meetin' ag'in."

"All right, Hickman — and thanks a-plenty. If yuh want me, I'll come to Salt Lake City for Stone's trial."

Hickman was riding off. He swung in his saddle, and for an instant the Rio Kid saw the gleam of white teeth through the mouth slit of the mask. Then the Mormons rode on, driving their captives before them. . . .

The following day, just before noon, General Grenville Dodge rode into Lost Canyon with thirty armed men from California.

The Rio Kid greeted him, shaking the great engineer's hand.

"We're exhausted!" Dodge panted, dismounting stiffly. "We've ridden without a break for thirty-six hours! I overtook the posse just before we came to where the Mormon's used to be. . . . You've been all right?"

Swiftly, the Rio Kid told him what had occurred.

"Good," said Dodge. "Stone was right, Rio Kid." From his pocket he drew the pendant which the Rio Kid had pressed on him the day they had met on the trail near the Mormon's. "You asked me to find out if these had value. They have. Stanford knows jewels. He says that the red one is a valuable fire opal, and he offered ten thousand dollars for it. The pearly blue one's larger but it's only worth a few hundred. It's a common opal. This third one is a turquoise and the small one's a precious ruby, not a garnet. This little trinket is worth about twelve to fifteen thousand."

The Rio Kid whistled. "No wonder Stone was so het up! Why, General, there's a whole caveful of them pebbles in back there! The stream washed out the mountain's innards and exposed 'em."

Later, after he had rested and eaten, Dodge examined the find. He could identify opals, turquoises, garnets and rubies, and a great lode of sparkling semi-precious gems.

The Rio Kid told the people of their luck.

"There's enough in here to make you all well-to-do, folks, and more besides!" he said. "Yuh won't have any trouble gettin' a start in California!"

The slope was gentler now, downhill, and the big wagons rolled easily. Beautiful green valleys and timbered hills showed before them. The people of the train gasped at the loveliness of the promised land.

"California!" cried Al Drew.

They paused to rest the horses, and got down. Jason Gray stood, an arm about Sue, who held Al Drew's big hand.

The Rio Kid with Jim Bridger and Mireles on their beautiful horses came riding back from the lead.

"Yuh're here, folks," he said. "This is California."

They had boxes filled with the semi-precious gems dug from the clay walls of the cave in Lost Canyon.

"We got to be ridin' back," said Bridger. "Dodge is waitin' for us in Utah."

The people tried to thank them.

"You take your share of the jewels," ordered Jason Gray.

"I got the pendant Sue gave me," said the Rio Kid. "That's enough for me."

The wild trails called. The three scouts took their leave. With sorrow the people watched the trio ride back, eastward for the Sierra passes. The Rio Kid turned, up on the hillside where the road swung into a cut, and waved, and they waved back. He recognized Sue's white kerchief fluttering in the breeze.

The Rio Kid set his shoulders. They rode through a clay-walled narrows, and before them loomed the mountains. And before the Rio Kid were the dangerous haunts he sought, that his restless blood must have.

The employees of Thorndike Press hope you have enjoyed this Large Print book. All our Thorndike and Wheeler Large Print titles are designed for easy reading, and all our books are made to last. Other Thorndike Press Large Print books are available at your library, through selected bookstores, or directly from us.

For information about titles, please call:

(800) 223-1244

or visit our Web site at:

www.gale.com/thorndike
www.gale.com/wheeler

To share your comments, please write:

Publisher
Thorndike Press
295 Kennedy Memorial Drive
Waterville, ME   04901